Sumikowa
The Haunting of Higanbana Heights

Tara A. Devlin

Sumikowa: The Haunting of Higanbana Heights
First Edition: June 2020

taraadevlin.com
© 2020 Tara A. Devlin

All rights reserved. No portion of this book may be reproduced in any form without permission from the publisher, except as permitted by U.S. copyright law. Names, characters, businesses, places, events, locales, and incidents are either the products of the author's imagination or used in a fictitious manner. Any resemblance to actual persons, living or dead, or actual events is purely coincidental.

DEDICATION

To all those creepy urban legends, ghost stories, and creepypastas that inspired these tales.

CONTENTS

Apartment 605 1

Apartment 302 19

Apartment 704 45

Apartment 804 62

Apartment 201 77

Apartment 503 94

Apartment 807 112

Apartment 404 130

Apartment 602 147

Apartment 308 163

Apartment 702 177

Apartment 206 195

APARTMENT 605

"Don't be ridiculous, there's no such thing as ghosts!

"Yeah, well, that's what my mother says, and what she says goes. And she also says we have to stay with my cousin for a few days while the Shinto priest does his thing."

"Are you for real?"

"I know, right? Like, I tried telling her that it's summer. You leave the windows open and of course things are gonna fly around the house. Wind does that, you know. Ugh, and I hate Toshiro. He's creepy…"

"He's your cousin, right?"

"Not by choice."

I laughed before I could stop myself. Ayaka, my best friend since elementary school, continued grumbling as I sank into the sofa of my new apartment. I grabbed the nearby remote and flicked on the TV. News played yet again of a serial killer in the nation's capital that took to cutting people's mouths open from ear to ear. They'd yet to catch the culprit, figure out a motive, or even connect the victims. They appeared, on the surface, to be utterly random.

The big city really was a terrifying place. Not that I'd gotten to see too much of it since my move from the countryside. Work ironically made sure of that.

"I said, are you even listening to me?"

I shook my head as Ayaka's voice brought me back. "Yeah, of course. That sucks."

"I know, right? I'm telling you, first opportunity I get, I'm coming to see you. You better be ready for me." A hint of amusement tinged her voice. It had been a long time since we had a girl's night out, just the two of us. Too long.

"You should have come to stay while the priest is doing... whatever he's doing to your house."

"Oh god, I wish, but we're wrapping up a big project at work and they need me there or something. Like they ever let me give any ideas, anyway."

I laughed again. I knew that feeling all too well. *"Natsumi, could you get me another coffee? Natsumi, do you have last Friday's financial report? Natsumi, could you order dinner for everyone, we're gonna be working late again."*

"I mean, who do I have to kill to get some respect, am I right?"

"The boss, probably."

"Oh man, I wish. But knowing him, he'd come back to haunt me and I'd be stuck with him forever." I could almost hear her shudder on the other end of the phone, and I smiled. I missed our conversations like this.

"Anyway, I gotta go, Mum's hassling me to pack some clothes so we can get out of the priest's hair. He won't even be here till tomorrow, god, she's such a slave driver."

"You really should move out, you know? You're 24, why are you living at home anyway?"

She scoffed. "Not all of us can get fancy big city jobs, you know? And I'm all my mother has left…"

"Yeah, I know…" An awkward silence filled the air.

"Look, I gotta go. We'll talk soon, okay?"

"Of course."

"Alright. Don't do anything I wouldn't do. Love ya!"

She hung up before I could get another word in, and I smiled. There was nothing she wouldn't do, so that didn't leave a whole lot. But on that note, I had work early the next morning too. Another day of being bossed around in my "dream big city job." Most days it just felt like my dream big city slavery with minimal perks…

* * *

My eyes slowly adjusted to the darkness as, confused, I looked around the room. I'd been living here for several months now, but still it seemed like every second night I woke up confused and disoriented, unsure of where I was. Only this time, something was different. Drastically different.

The curtains moved. They rose, as though reaching out for me, and then deflated, as though being sucked back into the wall. For a moment my heart skipped a beat, but then I remembered that I'd left the window open when I got into bed. One thing they didn't tell you about Tokyo was how hot it got during summer. Not just hot. Sweltering hot. The type that drowned you in your own sweat mere seconds after stepping out of a cold shower. I wiped my forearm against my head and both came away wet. Ugh.

I froze. Beyond the billowing curtain, in the corner of the room, a dark shadow loomed. It stood tall, human in shape, yet utterly motionless. I stared at it, my heart pounding like a jackhammer and sweat dripping down my face. Too frightened to move, too frightened to scream. A pair of statues, frozen in time. Who would be the first to kick-start it again?

The light switch hung above my bed. A piece of string, surprisingly old fashioned for an apartment that had supposedly been refurbished only a few years earlier. What happened to a simple switch? Yet in that moment I was grateful for the string; reaching out to grab it to illuminate the figure would be much easier than running for a switch on the wall.

The figure remained frozen, its eyes watching me. It knew. Somehow it knew that I was going to reach out for the light. That I was going to reveal it and that I would know it. Part of me wasn't even sure that I wanted to know, because unlike Ayaka's mother, I didn't believe in ghosts. Never had. As soon as I pulled that switch, I would know for certain who—or what—it was, and I wasn't sure if I was ready for the answer either way.

On the count of three. One. Two. I reached out for the switch and yanked it. A blinding light filled the room, and I screamed. I threw the blankets off the bed and stumbled into the opposing corner, putting as much distance between the figure and myself as I could. For what little good that might do.

I turned around. There was nothing there.

"...Huh?"

I looked around the room. Nothing. My bed in the middle, the bedside table next to it, the curtain billowing in front of an open window, and the light string swinging in the air beneath the bright fluorescent light. I was alone. I almost laughed.

Work must have been wearing me down good if I was so tired that I was seeing things. Just in case, I took another look around the room, ready to strike in case anything popped out, but I was completely and utterly alone. Alone in a city of millions, but more importantly, alone in my room in the middle of the night. And, for once, that was perfectly fine with me.

I crawled back into bed. Still a few more hours until I had to be at work, but the adrenaline had me wide awake. I pulled the string and darkness blanketed the room once more. Who was I kidding? I wasn't going to get any more sleep that night. I stared at the roof, listening for unnatural sounds that would inform me that I was wrong, that I really wasn't alone. There was nothing but the sounds of cars honking in the street outside and some yelling from another apartment. Another pleasant night in Higanbana Heights...

* * *

For three nights it continued. Around the same time, shortly after midnight, something woke me up and my eyes would immediately be drawn to the corner of the room. There it stood, the tall, dark figure looming in the corner. Always in the same position, always in the same stance. Watching me. Waiting for... something.

The first night I immediately grabbed the light string, hoping to catch it off guard. By the time my eyes adjusted to the sudden brightness, it was gone. The second time I watched it for a few minutes, waiting as my eyes adjusted to the darkness, but it stood frozen like a statue. Again when I gave in and pulled the light switch, it was gone.

The third night I contemplated shining my phone light on it, not giving it that split second of brightness to disappear, but to do that I'd have to reach out for my phone (which was charging on the bedside table), find the light app, and then open it, all before the dark figure knew what was going on. It was at that point that I realised I considered the dark shadow to be a real thing and shook my head.

No. Ghosts weren't real. They were stories told to scare children, and stories told to thrill bored people with the promise of death. Either for them or those around them. It didn't matter. Ghosts weren't real, and that thing in the corner certainly wasn't one either. It was my tired mind creating something that seemed real because the stress of the move and my new job were getting to me. That was all. So, on the third night, I didn't grab my phone, nor the light switch, and instead rolled back over and went back to sleep. This ghost, fake or otherwise, had taken enough of my time already.

I really should have grabbed that light switch.

* * *

"Nacchan, would you mind grabbing me another cup of tea? Thanks, dear."

My skin crawled. My friends from back home, they called me Nacchan. They had known me since I was a child. They were my friends. They had a right to call me that. When my boss did it? It felt gross and creepy and all I could do was smile and head to the tea room to grab him another cup of his beloved *sencha* tea.

"Here you are, sir." I painted on my best smile as I placed the cup before him.

"Ah, thank you, dear. Nobody else can make a cup quite like you, you know?" His grin turned lecherous, and he didn't even bother to hide his eyesight being drawn to my breasts. I bowed politely and stepped away, feeling his eyes burning into my backside as I retreated to my own desk. This was my life now, unless I wanted to return to the lack of jobs and lack of anything to do in the countryside. Put up with a few lecherous men at work, or put up with a complete lack of anything to do, ever. It sucked, but those were the choices.

APARTMENT 605

"So, do you really live at Higanbana Heights?" A middle-aged woman leaned in close as I sat down at my desk. I almost jumped out of my skin.

"I'm sorry?"

She leaned even closer, as though what she had to share was indecent for human ears. Other than mine, anyway.

"The section head Tanaka mentioned it the other day in passing. That you live in Higanbana Heights."

I couldn't hide the shock on my face, and before I could stop myself, my blood boiled. He was sharing my private information with others? Colleagues or not, that was still illegal. He grinned across the room at me, raising his eyebrows as he took another sip from his cup. My skin threatened to tear itself off my body in disgust.

"W-What about it?" I muttered, trying to focus on the computer in front of me. All I could see was red.

"Oh, you know. I heard the rumours, and I was wondering if they're true."

I turned to look at her, my eyebrows raised. What was her name again? The name-tag just above her breast pocket said "Nakata." Technically she was older than me, much older than me, but I had been at the company longer than her and if memory served me correctly, she came from a different line of work. This was her first time in an office. How did I even address her?

"What rumours, Nakata-san?" I went for the safe option.

She beamed, as though that was the answer she

was hoping for. "Ghosts, of course."

"...Ghosts?" My stomach sank.

"Yes. Everyone says Higanbana Heights is haunted. That's why the rent is so cheap. Even in Tokyo, nobody wants to live there. Well, is it?"

"Is it what?"

"Haunted?"

The rent was cheap, that was for sure. That was how I was able to get a place so easily. I didn't question it at the time, but now...

"I wouldn't know."

Her face fell. That wasn't the answer she was after, clearly. "Oh. Well. You should know, anyway. People say it's haunted, so I'd be careful if I were you."

The boss loudly sipped his tea. Loud enough for us to hear all the way across the room. I shuddered. I'd be hearing that sound in my nightmares. Maybe that dark shadow in the corner was really my mind manifesting my boss. Sickness rose inside me. There were plenty of things to worry about that didn't include rumours of my apartment building being haunted.

"I will, thank you," was all I could say.

"Nacchan!" Tanaka's voice rang out across the room. That rising sick feeling inside me got even worse. "Hey, Nacchan! Could you come here a moment? I need your help with something."

I pushed away from the desk and stood up, my shoulders slumping. "Coming, sir."

* * *

APARTMENT 605

The TV blared mindless noise in the background as I slumped on the couch. A message from Ayaka said that they were returning home, their ghostly infection finally gone. Nakata's words from earlier stuck in my mind.

"That's great. Apparently I live in a haunted apartment too," I replied.

"LOL! I told you that's why the rent's so cheap."

"Yeah, yeah. But honestly, I have been seeing something weird the last few days." I glanced over at the corner of the room. For a moment my heart jumped, but then I realised it was just the pot plant. Nothing there. Of course there wasn't.

"Like what?" The buzz of the phone startled me.

"I dunno, I guess I'm just tired. Sometimes when I wake up, I see something like a shadow in the corner of my room."

"Maybe you have a stalker, haha!"

"Don't be stupid."

"You do live in Tokyo after all~"

I sighed. *"Maybe you should send that priest my way."*

"Bit far for that, but if you're serious, I'm sure Tokyo has plenty who could come visit for you."

Was I serious? My phone said it was 11 p.m. Usually I'd be getting ready for bed around now, but instead the TV blared and I was doing everything I could to stay awake. The sooner I went to bed, the sooner I'd see that thing again, whatever it was… and the sooner I'd have to go back to work again as well. I shuddered, remembering the boss resting his hand on my shoulder earlier as he spoke to me, giving it a not-so-gentle squeeze.

"I'm not sure I'm cut out for this place," I typed. I looked at the text for a few moments and then deleted it. *"Yeah, you're probably right."* I hit send.

"You okay?"

"Just tired."

"Get to bed. That's what I'm going to do in our newly clean and ghost-free house, haha! Talk soon!"

"Night."

I dropped the phone on the couch beside me. My skin crawled. I no longer felt alone in my own house and it sucked. Slapping my cheeks a few times, I tried to focus on the TV in front of me, but it wasn't working. Nakata's words danced through my head.

Everyone says Higanbana Heights is haunted.

I jumped. The door seemed to rattle. The nearby fan buzzed softly, blowing already hot air onto my face and doing little to kill the heat. This city was so hot at night, but more importantly... it was 11 p.m.

"Hello?"

I tunnel-visioned on the door. The door handle had just rattled. I wasn't imagining it. I had seen it, for real.

"Hello?" I called out again. No response. I stood up, sweat running down my face, and took one step towards the door. My heart climbed into my throat and beat violently. Another step. I waited with bated breath for the handle to rattle again. Still nothing. I closed the distance and pressed my eye to the peep hole as gently as possible, fearing what I might see on the other side.

Nothing.

I let out the breath I didn't realise I'd been holding. Yeah. No. It was time to go to bed. I couldn't keep carrying on like this, jumping at every sound, every movement out of the corner of my eye. Some sleep would do me a world of good.

***

The sticky heat woke me up, and my eyes immediately went to the corner. I waited for my eyes to adjust, but it was just a wall. Nothing there. I almost laughed in relief. See? Just exhaustion, nothing more. Maybe a little stress from my shitty job and moving to a new city from a much, much smaller village. I relaxed back into the bed and closed my eyes, waiting for sleep to claim me once more.

My eyes shot open. Was that a… It sounded like something toppling over in the kitchen. I climbed out of bed and approached the bedroom door. It was slightly ajar, how I always left it in this heat. Pressing my face to the gap, I peered down the hall to the kitchen.

Nothing. Nothing I could see, anyway. The door opened with a slight creak, and I froze. Still nothing. No noise, no ghost, just me standing in my pyjamas by the door like a moron.

I padded down the hall and stuck my head around the corner. A cup lay on the floor. Well, I definitely hadn't left that there when I went to bed. I scanned the room, but nothing else seemed out of the ordinary. The curtain billowed above the sink.

The wind. It had to be.

I stopped. The hairs on my arms stood on end, and my breath caught in my throat. I blinked a few times, unsure if I was seeing correctly or if the darkness was creating monsters in my mind again.

A dark figure stood in the corner, unmoving. No, not again. My head pounded. *Just leave me alone*, I wanted to scream. *Whoever, whatever you are, get out of my house!* Instead, I stared at it, waiting for it to move. Would it rush me with a demonic screech? Would it fade into the wall? Would it smile as it disappeared, its curse laid and I now unable to escape it?

One minute passed. Two minutes. My legs began to shake under the pressure of forcing myself to stand as still as possible. I blinked, sweat dripping into my eyes and my vision blurring. The figure seemed to sway back and forth, as though standing behind a massive heat wave radiating off the floor.

How stupid I must have looked, standing at the end of my hall in the middle of the night staring at something on the other side of the room. I had to be up for work again in a few hours, and Tanaka would not give a shit that I was up half the night staring at a ghost. Then again, maybe realising that I was batshit insane would turn him off and make him leave me alone. I almost laughed. Almost. Except terror continued its hold on me and I was too scared to even twitch a finger muscle.

The light switch. A string hung above a tiny table in the middle of the room. The apartment wasn't big enough for a dining room, so the kitchen doubled as both. I would have to leap forward and fumble through the darkness to reach it. The shadow continued to stand stock-still across from me. Watching me. Waiting to see what move I would make.

Everyone says Higanbana Heights is haunted. Everyone could take a dive off a cliff. This wasn't what I signed up for when I moved here. I took the quietest, deepest breath I'd ever taken, allowing air to slowly fill my lungs as I readied myself. This couldn't go on all night. Now or never. Reach for that light string. Illuminate the figure. Find out once and for all what it really was.

One.

Two…

Three!

I leapt forward, my shin colliding with the table leg as my arm fumbled for the string. Any part of it would do. Something grazed my arm and I grabbed it, almost yanking the string out of the roof. Bright light flooded the room, burning my eyes. I screamed and stumbled back a few steps, my arms up and ready to protect myself as I clenched my eyes shut.

I waited. And waited. Nothing attacked. Nothing screamed. Nothing dragged me forcefully to the other side. I opened my eyes and lowered my arms. I stood alone in the kitchen, a cup on the floor and the curtains billowing softly in the intense heat. I almost felt like an idiot, except the hairs on the back of my neck refused to go down, and unease settled in the pit of my stomach.

A Shinto priest, huh? That was sounding less and less like a stupid idea…

* * *

I snuck into the bathroom during my lunch break and looked up the nearest shrine. A quick call and explanation of my problem and, surprisingly, the priest agreed to come out that very same night. There was an audible gasp when I said "Higanbana Heights" and my stomach sank. If even the priests were scared of the rumours, then…

Exhaustion and fear made it difficult to focus throughout the rest of the day, and I did my best to avoid conversation with Nakata. Tanaka was a little more difficult, and he seemed to enjoy my inability to fight off his advances even more. Nobody in the office made any attempts to help as he placed his hand around my waist and walked me back to my computer after requesting I make him yet another cup of tea, and seeing the cup only reminded me of the night before. I didn't want to go home, but I didn't want to stay at work either. Maybe a return to the countryside actually would do me some good. If Ayaka's house was now as ghost-free as she said it was, then…

The priest was waiting for me when I got home. 9 p.m. Tanaka had insisted everyone do overtime again for a big upcoming project, and that meant the office ladies as well, of course. The priest bowed as I approached, and I returned the gesture.

"You are Ms Yamada?"

"That's me, yes."

"You can call me Takeda. This is your apartment?"

Takeda sounded so… normal. I was expecting

something more "exotic," like, I dunno, Ryugu or Tsukumo. I nodded as he pointed to my door. He looked it over and then back to me. "Shall we go in?"

I nodded, taking my key out and fumbling with the handle. I opened the door and let him inside first. He removed his shoes, entered the lounge, and scanned the room.

"Would you mind waiting outside first?" he asked, his eyes scanning the roof and then running down along the walls.

"Uh, y-yes, of course."

He turned back and smiled. "Thank you."

This was stupid. Watching the holy man work his way through my house, looking at invisible things and nodding or shaking his head as he went, I started to regret calling him out. Had I really let exhaustion bring me this far?

I opened my mouth to say something, but he disappeared down the hall. I sighed. I leaned against the railing and looked over the edge. Six floors up. The wind was almost incessant up here, but it was still stinking hot. Sweat made my uniform cling to my skin. I just wanted to go inside, shower, have a beer, and then go to bed. Forget any of this had ever happened.

The priest exited the house a few minutes later, a troubled expression on his face.

"What is it?" My stomach dropped. Had he really found something? He closed the door behind him and held his arm out, urging me to walk with him. I felt sick. He'd really found something, hadn't he? They weren't lying. These apartments were haunted, and I just happened to rent one. I was living with a ghost.

"There's no ghost," he said. I stopped in my tracks and laughed before I could stop myself.

"Wait, what?"

He turned to look back at the apartment, as though confirming we were a safe distance away. He looked me straight in the eyes.

"Do you live alone?"

I tilted my head. "Of course I do."

"Any friends often come to spend the night?"

"No..."

"None at all?"

I shook my head. What was he getting at?

"Ma'am, your apartment isn't haunted, at least as far as I can tell. But..."

"...But what?"

"I think you should call the police and perhaps find somewhere else to spend tonight."

My head spun. I was even more confused than before.

"I don't under—"

"You're not being haunted by a ghost, ma'am. Now, please keep calm, and listen to me very carefully."

How could I keep calm? He wasn't making sense. A million thoughts ran through my mind, too many to keep up with.

"There was a man in your closet."

...A what? My mind stopped. All thoughts ground to a screeching halt.

"I've been to buildings like this before. It's unknown to most residents, but there are ducts in the roof that connect the apartments. The crawl space is small, but it's possible for a human to fit through them. There's one in your kitchen and another in your room. In your closet, to be more precise."

"In my closet...?"

He nodded. "Ma'am, it's not a ghost, and he's still in there. You should call the police. Immediately."

Perhaps it was time to give Ayaka a call. The big city really wasn't worth it anymore...

APARTMENT 302

"I'M HOME!" I DROPPED MY bag on the ground as I walked in and collapsed on the couch. There was a knock in the kitchen. I smiled. "And how was your day?" A brief silence before another knock. One knock for "good." I'd come to learn that over the last few weeks.

Grabbing the remote, I turned the TV on and sank further back into the couch. "How was my day? Awful. Just awful." I mindlessly flicked through the channels and I could almost feel the couch next to me depress. I closed my eyes for a moment and smiled. If I tried hard enough, I could almost feel her hand slowly sliding over mine as well.

"I'm telling you, the professor is working us like dogs. Only, dogs get better pay and food out of it."

My previous apartment building had been scheduled for demolition only a month into my final year at university. Crazy, right? This was the only place my parents were able to find on such short notice, and it was considerably further from school than the last place. Still, this one did have its benefits. If you could call them that.

"But enough about that. I deal with his slave driving all day. Is there anything you wanna watch, Sakura?" I'd taken to calling her Sakura because the first day I noticed her presence—again, I was just assuming it was a "her"—also happened to be the last day of the cherry blossoms blooming in the city. They had lasted extra-long this year, as though waiting for this particular moment before they finally passed on.

I flicked through the channels until I heard a knock on the coffee table before me. This was the one she wanted. A bunch of comedians and other untalented "talents" sat in rising rows watching ghost videos sent in by viewers. I raised an eyebrow.

"Bit on the nose, ain't it?"

No response.

"Well, you picked it. Don't come crying to me when you feel like they've depicted you badly."

To be honest, I hated ghost videos. I hated horror films, I hated horror games, I hated whenever my friends asked me to come visit an abandoned building with them at night because they wanted a cheap thrill. I hated all of it. Which was why it surprised me so much that when I first learnt of Sakura's presence, I felt... almost relieved. I hated being alone most of all, and now I no longer was! But unlike other roommates, she was clean, she was quiet, she didn't eat my food, she listened to everything I had to say without complaining, and she didn't clog up the drain with her hair, either. The perfect roommate.

Well, almost.

"Hey, Sakura."

Silence.

"Don't you ever wish that you could talk?"

A brief silence before a gentle knock on the table. I knew it.

"You know all about me, but I know so little about you."

It felt awkward sometimes, talking to an empty room and expecting an answer but knowing I'd never get one. That was how people talking to their pets probably felt, I guessed. But Sakura was no pet.

"There's so many things I want to ask you. Who are you? Why are you here? How old are you? What did you do? How did you..." My voice trailed off. That probably wasn't something she wanted to remember, and I regretted it the instant the words touched my lips.

Silence greeted me.

"Yeah, I know. My bad. We should just watch the show, yeah? I'll quit my idiotic ramblings..."

I closed my eyes as the impending jump scare approached and something soft tickled my neck. Sakura was resting her head against me. I knew it.

How lucky was I? The perfect roommate...

* * *

"I'm telling you guys, you gotta come around and check this out."

At school the next day I made the decision to finally introduce my friends to her. I couldn't keep hiding this any longer. Besides, I'd been getting too many questions over the last few weeks. "What are you smiling so much about, Toshiyuki?" "You got a new girl or something?" "Spill the deets, who's the mystery lady?" On and on, they wouldn't quit. It was time everyone saw the truth for themselves.

"Your apartment is haunted?" Jiro's eyebrow raised so high it threatened to fly off his face.

"What? You guys are the ones always dragging me around to haunted places I don't wanna see. Now you're questioning me?"

"Yeah, but... that's just for fun. Nobody actually thinks there are any ghosts there, right?" He looked around at the others for confirmation. They all nodded. "Why do you think we go there in the first place?"

Now I was confused. "You... go to haunted places because you don't want to see ghosts...?"

"Exactly."

"What?"

"What?"

I blinked rapidly and shook my head. Yuki smiled and placed her hand on my shoulder. "I believe you. Let's go."

I couldn't stop the grin from forming on my face... for various reasons.

"I wanna see whether this ghost is for real or not." She smiled.

* * *

Five of us stood before my apartment door. "I don't know how she'll react to other people, so, be gentle…"

Jiro rolled his eyes. Yuki smiled.

"Be gentle… It's a *ghost*…"

I narrowed my eyes and turned the key.

"I'm home!" I said as I opened the door. Just like always. I stood aside and let everyone in, closing the door behind them.

"Nice place," Yuki said.

"I had no idea you lived *here*," Eiji chimed in.

"Here?"

"Higanbana Heights." He said it as though that solved everything.

"Uh…"

"You haven't heard the stories?"

"Should I have?"

"You're the one who hates ghosts, man, not me."

"What stories?"

"This whole place is supposed to be more haunted than Hell, man. I heard that this place is even a gateway to the other side. That's why so many apartments are always empty, and why people come and go so often."

"…Yet you refuse to believe that I might be living with a ghost?" They were making even less sense than usual.

"Hey man, I never said anything. That was Jiro."

"Pfft," Jiro replied. "The whole city's full of haunted buildings like this, if you believe the stories. Nobody would be able to move for all the ghosts if you believed everything you hear."

"Well, they are invisible. So maybe they are all

around us, but we just can't feel them?" Yuki suggested.

"No, no, you can definitely feel them!" I said. All eyes turned to me. Jiro's other eyebrow raised this time. "No, not like that! Just! Oh, shut up. Look. Listen. Sakura?"

I called out towards the kitchen. She was usually in there when I got home. Whenever I announced my presence it would take a few seconds before I received a gentle rap in reply.

One... Two... Three... Several seconds passed in awkward silence.

"Great haunting, mate. Top notch. Would visit again."

"Shut up!" I walked into the kitchen, my heart pounding like crazy. Did she not like visitors? Was she shy? "Sakura?" Still no response. The other four looked at me, waiting for something, anything, to happen.

"I... I dunno. Maybe she's shy."

"Your ghost is shy?"

"I don't know! This is the first time for me too, you know!"

"I think you've been working a bit too hard lately, man. Maybe you should ask the professor for a few days off, or..."

"It's not that!" My voice came out louder than intended and everyone jumped. "It's not. She's here. She's real. She's just... I don't know. Maybe she doesn't like other people. Maybe she's just used to me because I live here. I don't... I don't know."

I collapsed on the chair by the table. Yuki crossed the room and sat down beside me, resting a hand on my own. It was the same feeling as when Sakura did it. Butterflies jumped in my stomach. She was real. I knew she was.

"It's okay. I believe you. I wouldn't come out for a group of strangers just to be treated like a show pony either."

Of course. That was it! Here I was trying to parade her to my friends like an animal at the zoo. Of course she wouldn't appear! How stupid of me. How thoughtless and callous. I'd be lucky if she spoke to me again all night after this.

"Well, you guys are here now. Wanna order some dinner?"

"Oooh, pizza!"

"Supreme for me!"

"I want Hawaiian!"

"You filthy monster."

"What?"

"Get that pineapple off my pizza and where it belongs. In the trash."

"I don't think the trash could fit anything else in it, it's already full with your dumb ass."

Yuki moved to the corner of the kitchen to order while the others argued. 'I'm sorry, Sakura.' I thought, wondering if she could even hear it. 'Looks like it's going to get a bit noisy tonight.'

* * *

Three days passed without word from Sakura. As much as I hated to admit it, I was beginning to get worried. "I'm home!" I'd yell each time I got home, only now there was no response. No knock. No gentle gust of wind brushing through my hair as she passed. No soft pressure on my hand as we sat on the couch and watched TV together. I was truly alone, and for all my fear of ghosts... that frightened me even more.

But on the upside, things with Yuki were going great. We chatted the whole night they all came over, and we'd been texting more ever since as well.

"You home?" My phone buzzed, and I smiled when I saw the message.

"I am. You?"

"Yeah. Still no response from your ghostly friend?"

It was hard to tell if she was making fun of me at times, but she seemed genuine.

"Nothing."

"I'm sorry. We probably shouldn't have come over. Maybe so many of us scared her."

"It's cool. I shouldn't have tried to show her off like a circus animal anyway. My fault."

"You were excited. I get that."

She was so kind and understanding. My heart skipped a beat.

"Kinda lonely here without her now."

"Like you lost a girlfriend? ;)"

I laughed despite myself. She didn't have to put it that way. Although... I shook my head.

"Like I lost a friend. A roommate." The words dug like daggers even as I typed them, as though I were betraying Sakura. No. She was the one who'd left me. I tried to introduce her to my friends, and she left. This was her fault. Not mine.

"Yeah, that's gotta suck. Hey, you wanna stop by that sushi place near school after class tomorrow? I heard they have a student special on Thursday afternoons."

"Yeah, sure. Sounds great!"

"Great! See you then."

I put my phone down and leaned back into the couch. Was this... a date? An honest to god real date? With a real woman? I couldn't wipe the smirk from my face. Grabbing a can of cheap beer from the fridge, I kicked back to watch what *I* wanted on the TV for once. No ghosts. No stupid comedians that weren't even funny. I found a documentary and let it play as my mind wandered.

A date. Go me.

* * *

"So, after what Eiji said the other night, I looked into the history of Higanbana Heights," Yuki said between bites of sushi.

"Yeah?" The words weren't really entering my head. I was too distracted by the movement of her lips.

"Apparently, the building itself is pretty old. I couldn't find exact records, but from what I could dig up, it was first built sometime after the war, and it's been renovated several times since then."

"Uh huh."

"There's no information on the actual owner, looks like it's being managed by a paper company, which is pretty suspicious if you ask me."

"Sure is, yeah."

"Are you listening to me?"

"What? Yes. Of course. Why wouldn't I be?"

"My face is up here."

I blushed. "Sorry, I zoned out..."

"Clearly."

"You were saying?"

"I'm saying that it's pretty suspicious, is all. Why are they hiding who owns the building? It's also been through several name changes over the years, the small amount of information I could dig up was because I looked up the address, not the name."

"Truly fascinating."

"Toshiyuki."

"Yes?"

"At least pretend you're listening."

I swallowed the sushi in my mouth and smiled. "Believe it or not, I actually was."

"What did I just say?"

"The building is run by a paper company and it's suspicious that you couldn't find any other information."

Yuki narrowed her eyes at me. "You're smarter than you look, huh?"

"Should I be offended?"

"I dunno. Should you?"

I narrowed my eyes in return. She smiled and I burst out laughing, unable to hold the expression any longer.

"So, nothing about crazy serial murderers or mysterious priestly visits?"

She shook her head. "I was able to find a few incidents in the publicly listed records, but honestly, it's like they've tried to scrub the building's existence from memory. Which makes me even more suspicious."

"Maybe there's a good reason for that."

"Huh?"

"I mean, Tokyo's a big city with a long history. There have no doubt been murders, suicides, and other crazy incidents in every building all over the city. I doubt this one is special in that regard."

She eyed me for a moment, her sushi forgotten. "So you're saying you have no problem living in a haunted building?"

An imaged floated by. A silhouette. A shape that didn't exist. Gentle curves and flowing hair. I'd never actually seen them, but my mind filled in the blanks. Sakura. A feeling I couldn't explain spread throughout my chest.

"Would that be so bad?"

Yuki scoffed. "I dunno about you, but I don't want to live with any ghosts." She picked up another piece of sushi and threw the entire piece in her mouth. She chewed a few times, swallowed, took a drink of tea and then looked me in the eye. "Is this about your ghost friend?"

"She's real, you know." The words sounded pathetic before they even left my mouth. A very real and very beautiful girl sat before me, and here I was muttering about a ghost no-one else had ever seen. But she was real. I knew it.

Yuki rested her hand on top of mine again. The familiar butterflies in my stomach grew. "I believe you."

I didn't know what to say, so I grabbed some

more sushi and shoved it in my mouth. She removed her hand and a pang shot through my heart. What on earth was going on? And why had Sakura abandoned me?

* * *

"I'm home," I said as I stepped through the door. I threw my bag down by the TV cabinet and collapsed on the couch. 11:30 p.m. I waited, but as usual there was no response. Sighing, I grabbed the remote and turned the TV on. Some noise to fill the void, though it could do little to fill the void in my heart.

I closed my eyes and lay my head back, hitting the wall behind me. Maybe a drink or two before bed. I bought some cheap one cup sake at the store a few days ago, that should still be in the fridge. I couldn't afford much else these days, not unless I wanted to get a job on top of everything else. My insides squirmed. Nah, I'd rather go without food first.

My heart stopped. A familiar warm feeling slid over my hand as it rested on the couch. I opened my eyes and stared at the roof. I couldn't move. If I did, I might scare her away. My heartbeat pounded in my ears and sweat trickled down the side of my face. This building was so hot. Unnaturally hot, even for a big city summer.

I squeezed the air. I couldn't quite grab her hand, but the gesture would convey my feelings. A presence leaned back against the couch next to me.

"I missed you…" My voice cracked, the words

coming out barely above a whisper. "I'm sorry."

There was no response, but she was there. That was enough. I turned to look. The couch was empty, but if I squinted and tried hard enough, I could almost see an outline. Or maybe I was just telling myself that. Either way, I smiled. Sakura was back.

"I'm sorry I brought all those people back here the other night. I didn't know that you'd be so upset. If I had—"

A pressure squeezed my hand. "It's okay," she was trying to say.

"They're my friends. I just wanted you to meet them."

Another squeeze.

"They're good guys, you know? They wouldn't do anything to—"

An even harder squeeze.

"I know. I'm sorry. I should have asked first."

A brief pause before a softer squeeze. Apology accepted. We watched TV in silence for a while, but thoughts soon flooded my head. The building was run by a paper company. It was as though they had tried to scrub the building's existence from memory. Yuki's words played over and over in my head. Did Sakura know anything about that? Did I even want to know? I only had to stay here less than a year before I graduated and then I could move on. Perhaps it would be for the best not to pry. Let sleeping dogs lie, don't stir the hornet's nest, etc etc.

Yet the seeds had been planted. As I drifted off to sleep, images of the walls of my apartment turning red seeped into my mind...

* * *

"Yuki, can I ask you something?"

"Shoot."

Several days had passed with terrible nightmares and little sleep. A big test was coming up soon and with graduation close at hand, I couldn't let anything slip up now.

"I've been having these... I guess dreams lately."

"Okay. Is that why you look like shit?"

I tried to force a smile. "That's my natural look, but thanks."

She grinned but kept her eyes focused on me, waiting for me to continue. A joke. That was what friends did. They joked.

"Anyway, this is gonna sound stupid, but... I think someone was murdered in my apartment."

"Murdered? As in, recently, or...?"

"As in I dunno. I keep having these dreams. The walls, they're red, and someone's screaming and I wake up covered in sweat and... I sound stupid, don't I?"

"Absolutely."

"I'm sorry..."

"But I believe you."

I perked up. "You do?"

She nodded. "I told you, I think some weird shit has gone down there. Murder would be the least of it."

"Oh, thank god."

"I dunno about that, but I'd say those dreams are

no coincidence. My grandma spent a few nights in a hotel once when she was younger and she had all these gnarly dreams. Screams, smells, sights, the whole shebang. It was like she was there herself, she said, but unable to do anything. She found a talisman behind one of the paintings on her final day, and when she asked the front desk about it on her way out, they admitted it was there for a reason but wouldn't say why. Weird shit happens that we can't explain. The others might not believe that stuff, but I've seen enough to make me question things."

Relief like nothing I'd ever experienced before flooded through me. "That leads me to my next question."

"Yes."

"Sorry?"

"Yes. I'll come around and have a look with you again. That's what you were going to ask, right?"

How did she do that? "Maybe..."

"Tonight sound good?"

"Sure..."

"Great! See you then."

* * *

Yuki showed up right on schedule. I left the lab early, and she was waiting on the ground level for me when I got home. "I didn't really want to go up alone," she said. "This place still bugs me out."

Silence filled the elevator as we rode up, and my heart pounded in my throat as we approached the door. How would Sakura react? After the first time I brought friends over, she disappeared. Maybe she didn't like big groups? Would a single person be okay? Only one way to find out.

I put the key in the lock and turned to Yuki. "Yuki…"

"I won't do anything to antagonise your ghost friend, don't worry." She smiled and I couldn't help but return the gesture. There she went again. Reading my thoughts before I even knew what I wanted to say myself.

I turned the key and stepped inside. "I'm home!" A gust of hot wind blew over my face and I stepped aside to let Yuki in. "Yuki's here!" I added, just in case. The apartment remained silent. I shrugged, and Yuki stepped through the door. "Excuse me."

Yuki removed her shoes and stepped into the living room. She took a look around the room, taking it all in, and then walked into the kitchen.

"You got any *sake*?" she asked.

"Huh?" The question took me aback.

"Sake?" She opened the fridge and smiled. "Ah, there it is. I knew you'd have some." She removed a one cup sake and ripped the lid off.

"Hey!"

She took a big gulp, swished it around in her mouth for a moment and then swallowed with a grimace. She held the cup out towards me and jerked her head. "Drink some."

I grabbed it wordlessly and took a sip. It tasted like cheap sake. What else was she expecting?

"How is it?"

I shrugged. "Cheap. Why?"

"Take another sip. Focus on it."

I raised an eyebrow but I did as she said. The sake hit my tongue and I swished it around a little like she did. Cheap. Slightly bitter, but otherwise nondescript. I swallowed, and it burned as it went down, leaving almost a pungent, sickly sweet residue as it did.

…Huh.

Yuki smiled as she saw the recognition on my face.

"Eww. What is that?"

"Something my grandma taught me. There's definitely something here."

Not that I needed the confirmation, but I knew it.

"You can tell just from the sake?"

She nodded. "Old shaman trick. Sadly a lost art these days, or so my grandma says. The question is, what do you want to do now?"

I furrowed my brow. "What do you mean?"

The TV suddenly turned on behind me and I jumped, spilling the sake on the floor.

"That." Yuki pointed. She took a step back and pressed herself against the sink. I screamed as the TV suddenly exploded. Smoke wafted into the air as the insides fizzled out and the room fell silent again.

"What the…"

The apartment went dark. The lights in the living room and kitchen exploded at the same time. They didn't go out. They exploded. Shards of glass shattered to the floor and rained on us.

"Yuki!"

"I'm fine," she replied. She hadn't moved from the kitchen sink. My eyes slowly adjusted to the darkness. She was looking at something I couldn't see in the living room.

"Yuki?"

"I noticed it the first time we came here," she said, taking a step towards me but not removing her eyes from whatever she was looking at over my shoulder. "I wasn't sure, but I felt something when we entered. Then it disappeared."

"...Sakura?"

She nodded.

"Is she...?"

She nodded again.

Hands slid around my waist. Hands I couldn't see or even feel, but they were there. They clung tighter and pulled me back.

"...Yuki...?" The hands were the least of my concerns. I couldn't tear my eyes off the walls. They darkened, streaks of red leaking from all over, a pungent metallic tang filling the air with them.

"Stay calm."

"How am I supposed to do that? The walls are—"

"I know. Stay calm."

She held her hand up, her fingers positioned in a gesture I'd never seen before.

"What are you—"

"Shh."

The grip around my wrist tightened. Blood seeped from the walls to the floor. Papers on the coffee table swirled and tore in the air. A piece flew past my head, cutting my cheek as it made its way towards Yuki.

"Yuki!"

The paper disintegrated into a tiny puff of flames. The room grew hotter, darker, wetter.

"S-Sakura…" My voice trembled. The pressure against my waist was so tight it felt like I was going to pop. "Y-You're hurting me…"

"Her name's not Sakura."

"What?"

Yuki took a step closer. Something pulled me a step backwards.

"Sachie, right? Your name is Sachie."

The pressure around my waist held firm, but for the first time stopped getting tighter.

"S-Sachie?" I tried the word for the first time. It felt foreign on my lips. I was so used to calling her Sakura. Who was Sachie? Sachie was a stranger to me.

The grip loosened slightly.

Emboldened, I swallowed my nerves and tried again. "Sachie? I'm sorry. I didn't know your name, so I—"

She pulled me back again. Blood seeped into the carpet. I jumped as the TV fell off the cabinet and fell with a wet thud.

"What is it that you want?" Yuki asked. She matched each step Sachie dragged me back with one of her own.

"Can you… can you hear her?" I'd never heard Sakura… Sachie's voice. Never seen her. Nothing. I just felt something there and I'd given it a name. A life. Feelings and a personality that only existed in my mind. But she was real. She was real, and she was dragging me towards a bloody pool gathering in the middle of the room.

Yuki said nothing. She continued her attentions towards Sachie. "Let me help you."

The pool of blood was getting larger, and the grip around my waist tightened once more.

"I'm not sure she wants help…" My voice cracked. "Oh god…"

All this time I'd had a romantic image of Sakura in my head. The girlfriend of my dreams. Always there at the end of a long day to listen to my complaints. To give me a comforting hand and reassuring presence when I was exhausted and confused. My own private partner that nobody knew about but me.

That woman didn't exist. That woman was now trying to drag me into a pool of blood that led who knew where whilst my apartment fell apart around me.

"Something terrible happened to you here, I understand that." Yuki took a step closer, and then another. The movements were almost imperceptible, except for the fact my senses were running a million miles an hour and I could probably see the fluttering of a fly's wings if one passed by. The absurdity of the thought almost made me laugh. Almost. I was still being dragged towards a pool of blood, after all.

"But I can't let you take him."

The squeezing around my waist intensified. "I don't… think… she's listening…"

Images flashed in my mind. An unknown woman, her hair pinned up and fastened with gorgeous pendants. A man, knocking on the door. My door. No, not mine. An older style with no peep hole. Screams. Blood. Walls turning red. Wails. Furniture exploding. Hands. So many hands. Coming out of the floor, the roof, the walls…

"No!"

I struggled anew, realising what was going on. Yuki's eyes opened wide for a moment before she renewed her focus on whatever was behind me.

"Someone hurt you, I get that. You're angry. You want revenge. But Toshiyuki didn't do it. This has nothing to do with him…" She took another step closer, and then another, her feet sliding across the floor.

"No!" I screamed again. "No, Yuki! That's not it!"

She narrowed her eyes, briefly flicking them to me before returning to the space above my shoulder.

"What?"

Screams. A man's screams. Not Sakura… no, Sachie. Not her. The blood coating the walls. The floor. The roof. It wasn't Sachie's blood.

It was his.

As her grip tightened, more images flooded my brain. I saw them play out before me like a movie. Could Yuki see the same thing, or was it something Sachie was unknowingly projecting into my head? The man, a suitor by the looks of him, smiled as Sachie opened the door. It was my apartment, but different. Older. Much older. Perhaps when the building had first been built.

She let him in, and he handed her a single flower. He sat down on the couch and Sachie returned with two drinks. One for him, one for her.

APARTMENT 302

She handed the man his cup, sat down next to him, and smiled. He downed it without a second thought. I gulped. He didn't even notice it. The strange taste. I could feel it sliding down my throat, burning the entire way down.

She drugged him.

Sachie started screaming. I couldn't understand a word she was saying. My vision blurred, just like the man's. Something glinted in the light. Pain tore through my bicep. My thigh. My stomach. My neck. Bright red splatters coated the wall. The floor. The roof. I fell to the ground. No, the man, not me. Or was it me?

I gurgled, choking on my own blood. Laughter. A woman's laughter above me. More words I couldn't understand. Darkness. A cold darkness washing over me. Drops. Drops on my head. My own blood, dripping from the roof where it had landed. Wetness surrounding me, threatening to swallow me whole. Body going numb. Laughter fading in my eyes. World going black.

"No!" The sound of my own screams brought me back. I struggled frantically and Yuki leapt. She whipped something out of her pocket and I slid in the blood coating the floor. I didn't care. An unholy scream ripped through the apartment as the grip around my waist loosened and sticky liquid splattered my face as I struggled to squirm free of it. I ran on all fours towards the kitchen and, when I turned back, widened my eyes in horror.

There she was. Sachie. Not my Sakura. No, she was never my Sakura. A tall, beautiful woman, with elegant cheekbones and big round eyes screamed and hissed, blood whirling around her. Dark veins tracked her face, her arms, anywhere with bare skin. Her skin... her skin was grey, almost black, and looked like it might crumble into pieces at any moment.

Yuki continued tossing something that looked like salt and water on her from separate vials and it fizzled as it hit her skin. Her eyes, pure red, turned to stare at me in the darkness, hateful and full of rage. She never meant to comfort me. She was merely biding her time, waiting until she could do the same to me as she had that man. She wasn't a ghost stuck to the apartment she'd been murdered in. She'd already been here a long time before this building even existed. The newly built physical walls kept her in, but she'd already been here long before that. Too long... and she wouldn't stop.

Another scream tore through the apartment. The walls themselves seemed to shake, enough that I feared they might collapse in on us. Yuki chanted something and moved her arms and fingers in an elaborate dance as she threw the last of her bottles on the demon woman. A bright orange light filled the room as the woman burst into flames.

"Oh god..."

An inhuman screech pierced my ears, and the woman sank into the floor. She didn't collapse; she sank into it. Disappearing into the pool of blood. It sucked her in, first up to her ankles, then her knees, then her thighs...

"Toshiyuki!"

Bile rose in my throat. Pain flooded my head and my vision blurred.

"Toshiyuki!" Yuki stood before me, shaking my shoulders.

"Huh? What?"

"We gotta get outta here! Now!"

I let her drag me from the apartment, my skin crawling as we slid along the wall to pass by her. My Sakura. She never was my Sakura. Sakura didn't exist. There was only Sachie.

The blood-curdling screams continued behind us as Yuki flung the door open and we tumbled out onto the balcony. The door slammed shut behind us and the screams continued for another few seconds followed by a loud bang and then silence. Unnatural silence.

Yuki rested her head against the balcony and sighed. A resident coming up the stairs stopped once she hit the landing and saw us. Both of us were soaked head to toe in blood.

"Uh…"

"Painting accident," Yuki muttered, exhausted. The tenant nodded and kept walking, casting a nervous sidelong glance back at us.

"Is… is she gone?" I could barely comprehend what had just gone down. Yuki shook her head.

"I'm not strong enough for that. I don't know if anyone is. You might want to think about finding a new place to stay for a while. I hope you didn't have anything important in there."

"Just my entire life."

She smiled. I tried to smile back. All I could taste was blood.

I turned to the side and threw up.

* * *

"She killed that man."
Yuki nodded.
"And she was going to kill me."
Yuki nodded again.
"I don't... I was so stupid."
I waited for her to refute me, but she nodded once more.
"How did she... who was she even?"
Yuki shrugged. I'd been staying with her family since the incident, and as it turned out, her entire family were shamans. Well, all the women, anyway. Her father smiled and patted me on the shoulder when we showed up, covered in blood, and silently led me to the bathroom. The matter-of-factness of it, and the tiny fact that he didn't even bother to ask what happened was perhaps the scariest part of all. This was *normal* to him. I shuddered.
"A spirit that powerful has to be old. Really old."
"Like, 50 years old, or...?"
"Add a zero."
I narrowed my eyes. I couldn't tell if she was joking or not.
"Why didn't she just kill me to begin with?"
Yuki shrugged again. "I imagine after so many years stuck in the same spot, you probably want a bit of excitement before you go in for the kill."
Did she have to put it like that? Even now I still felt like I was washing blood out of various crevices and holes in my body. And I didn't even know whose blood it was.
Yuki's dad sat down next to me and plopped a

large plate of pancakes in front of me. A large smile painted his face.

"Eat," he said. I eyed him a moment before grabbing the fork and stabbing it into the pancakes. Syrup slowly dribbled down them. They tasted delicious, but the man's grin unnerved me.

"Trust me, son. Sometimes it's better not to know." He patted my shoulder again and stood up, stretching and yawning before he left the room. "Trust me!"

"Can he see…?"

Yuki shook her head.

"But all of you can…?"

She smiled, her eyes flickering over my shoulder before returning to my face.

I shoved another forkful of pancakes into my mouth. Yeah. He had a point. Maybe it was best not to know.

APARTMENT 704

ANOTHER DAY, ANOTHER EMERGENCY.

"We need you in right away."

I closed my eyes and rubbed my temples. "I just got home from a 15 hour shift."

"And we need you in right away."

There was no sigh that would accurately convey my exhaustion.

"You can't get in Erika or Mei?"

"You think we'd be calling you if we could?"

Was I supposed to be offended by that? I was too tired to even care. 15 hours at one of the biggest hospitals in the country and I'd barely been home long enough to pour myself a glass of wine and they wanted me back for extra shifts. I hadn't had a day off in over two weeks. Why couldn't they get someone else in for once?

"Sure, I'll be in right away." The wine would have to wait.

"Make it snappy. Things are going crazy down

here."

The phone hung up, and I dropped my forehead to the table. Ugh. I would give my right arm for just a few hours of sleep. That was all. Not even a full night. A few simple hours would do.

Back to the grind…

* * *

I collapsed face-first on the bed. The softness threatened to swallow me whole. Suck me into another dimension of fluffiness and warmth and I welcomed it. Sadly it didn't, but the thought was nice enough.

Turning my phone off, I rolled over and let out the tired sigh that had been building. No more emergency shifts. They could get someone else to cover for once. My regular shift was supposed to start again in eight hours. They could find someone else if yet another emergency popped up.

A train had hit a bus in one of the more populated sections of the city and our hospital happened to be the closest. The impact had obliterated the bus, and we were left to put the human pieces back together again. It was like walking into a slaughterhouse. Passengers missing limbs. Passengers that had been crushed to a pulp. Passengers that were otherwise fine but had taken nasty cuts from all the broken glass and thus looked like they'd struggled out of a pool of blood. Which they had, I supposed.

The screams and sights and smells normally haunted my nightmares, but I was so exhausted that as I looked at the blank canvas of my roof, I felt nothing. Absolutely nothing.

The last thought that crossed my mind before sleep claimed me was how that tiny spot of black above my head extraordinarily stood out amongst the backdrop of pure white.

* * *

"What's the best thing to get rid of mould?"

"Mould?" Erika's eyes flickered up from the chart she was filling in.

"Yeah. I noticed a spot on the roof. My apartment is already shabby enough, can't have that spreading through it."

A sly smile grew on her lips. "You sure it's just mould?"

"What else would it be?"

"Oh, you know. A ghost or something. You've seen that movie, yeah?"

I stared at her blankly.

"The one with the... never mind."

"You know I don't have time for movies."

"And that's why you're a boring old lady nobody will ever love."

"You're the best friend a lady could ask for."

"I know. You could grab some mould killer from the store or something on your way home. If it hasn't spread, that would no doubt be good enough."

We finished our rounds and moved to the next room.

"It's summer, mould is common at this time of

year." I sounded like a child continuing the conversation Erika had already moved on from, but that was nothing to joke about. Ghosts in the roof? How stupid.

"Uh huh."

I pouted. Erika smiled.

"Even if you believe in ghosts, that doesn't make any sense."

"What doesn't?"

We entered the next room, and Erika started checking the patient charts again.

"Why would a ghost make a dark stain in the roof? Think about it. It doesn't make sense."

"Why not?"

"Well… it's a ghost. How does it make sense?"

"You're not making any sense."

"What?"

"What?"

I narrowed my eyes at her. She smiled and crossed off a few more boxes before moving to the next patient.

"People often say that they can see faces in stains, right? Like, on the wall, on the floor, the roof, wherever. It's just a coincidence, of course, but sometimes you really do come across one that looks exactly like a face and it makes you wonder. People say that if you find one that looks to be in pain, chances are good it's not just a coincidence. That there really is a spirit trapped in there."

"…That's stupid."

"Sure it is. Enjoy your new roommate."

I opened my mouth, but no words came out. Erika grinned and patted me on the shoulder as she passed by. "Some company might do you good, yeah?"

"What are you trying to say?" The words followed her back as she moved to the last patient in the room. I narrowed my eyes again. "The cheek… I'm perfectly happy by myself…"

"You really should get that checked out."

I jumped. The patient in the bed next to me stared at me, unmoving.

"I'm sorry?"

"Your mould problem. I used to be a plumber. Mould is no joke."

I forced a smile. "Yeah. Right. Of course. Thank you."

Erika snickered as we moved onto the next room.

* * *

"It *is* getting bigger. I knew it."

With my store-bought mould killer in hand, I aimed for the roof and sprayed a few times. Would this even work? I grabbed the most expensive brand, but they were likely all made by the same company anyway and just packaged differently. Maybe I should have gone for the cheap one. But just in case…

I gave a few more squirts and jumped off the bed. The spot was still small. No bigger than a 500 yen coin. Plenty of time to nip it in the bud before it spread.

Erika's words weighed on my mind more than I cared to admit. I didn't believe in ghosts. Who did? But… what if? What if the spot continued to get bigger. What if it started to look like a human face in agony, staring down at me in my bed, watching me each night as I slept? What then?

I shook my head. No. That was nonsense. Erika enjoyed poking fun at me, that was all. Well, I'd show her. I'd kill the mould before it had a chance to grow, and that would be that.

As I got into bed that night, I couldn't stop looking at it. Was it still getting bigger? It looked bigger. The more I focused on it, the harder it was to tell. No. My brain was convincing me it was bigger, nothing more. It was still the same size. Just a small patch of mould. It only looked bigger because I had sprayed it. That was the mould killer doing its job. Yeah.

How was it midnight already? I sighed and turned over. I had to get up early for work and here I was staring at a literal spot on my roof.

...But it stood out so much. Ugh. I wanted to get up there and scratch it off with my nails. That one spot marred the entire roof, and by extension the entire room. I tossed and turned, doing my best to ignore it, but in my mind's eye I could see the spot growing. Spreading out like veins. Forming a smiling face grinning down at me. No, a pained face, screaming at me for help.

Dammit. It was just mould. Just mould.

Black tendrils filled my dreams, spreading out from my roof and taking over my entire house before absorbing me into its dark depths...

* * *

"Dammit!"

I sprayed the mould over and over. It was no 500 yen coin anymore. It wasn't even a 1,000 yen note. The mould had spread to bigger than the size of my hand. This damn spray was only making it worse. On the upside, it didn't look like a face, but on the downside, the mould was spreading with unimaginable speed. At this rate I'd probably wake up tomorrow and the thing would be the size of a small child. I shuddered.

"I don't have time for this!" I sprayed it a few more times, placing the bottle on my bedside table and grabbing up the stuff I needed for work. If it was still there when I got back, well then I'd have to look into a professional. Mould that rampant would make the apartment itself dangerous to live in. I of all people knew that.

Erika looked at me expectantly as I got in.

"What?"

"Well?"

"Your mould problem."

"What about it?"

"It looking at you yet?"

"Huh?" My dreams of being swallowed by mould had left me even more exhausted than when I got into bed.

"Does it look like a face yet?"

"Go away, Erika."

Her smile grew even bigger. "You can come stay at my place if you want. We can look for a good exorcist together."

"Or I could use your face to clean it."

She scoffed. "Well, that's a bit rude." A smile

hid behind her lips.

"Seriously though, it's getting bigger. I'm not sure what to do."

"You tried the spray?"

I nodded.

"Hmm. That is a problem. Mould doesn't usually spread that quickly. Not that I'd know. We've never really dealt with it in our house."

"Because you don't deal with anything at your house, that's what you have maids for."

"What's that supposed to mean?"

"Exactly what it sounds like."

Erika narrowed her eyes at me. I narrowed mine in return.

"Ladies, ladies. Please." Mei stepped between us as though breaking up a fight. "Now, what's all this about ghosts?"

"It's not a ghost!" Exasperated, I finished putting on my uniform and left the nurse's room.

"She's got a ghost in her roof," Erika said behind me.

"It's not a ghost!" My voice came out louder than intended and several patients looked my way. I smiled and hurried down the hall. Erika and Mei's footsteps soon followed.

"A ghost? Really?"

"She lives in Higanbana Heights, you know. Of course it's a ghost."

"Oh my god, really? How did I go all this time without hearing that? That place is haunted up the wazoo."

Wazoo?

"I know, right? You'd think on a nurse's salary

she could afford to live somewhere a little less haunted."

"I can hear you, you know!" I stopped and turned around. Erika and Mei smiled in unison.

"You really should get that looked at," Mei said. "I knew someone who lived there once. A few years back. They had to move because things kept moving around their apartment, lights turning on and off, dishes falling out of the cupboard, all of it. Even priests don't wanna go near that place."

"Thank you for your concern, but for the millionth time, it's just mould."

"But are you sure?"

"Why wouldn't I be? What else could it be? And if you say a ghost, I swear to god I will slap you right across the face."

Erika and Mei looked at each other. "The ghost is making her feisty. No good."

"Oh my god…" Throwing my hands up in the air, I continued down the hall, leaving them standing there behind me.

"At the very least you should check the water tank on the roof!" Mei called out. "There could be a dead body in there!"

"How would that cause a stain in my roof?" I called back, not bothered to turn around.

"The spirits work in mysterious ways!" Mei's words echoed down the corridor. A few moments later their footsteps caught up behind me.

"Look, time to get to work. I've had my fill of mould and ghosts. Let's just do what we're here to be paid for, okay?"

Ghosts. Dead bodies in water tanks. Haunted

buildings. Seriously. We were all a little too old to be believing in that stuff anymore.

* * *

"It looks like a face."

I stood in the doorway to my bedroom, and a chill ran through me.

"You gotta be shitting me…"

No. Erika and Mei's teasing was getting to me, that was all. The patch had grown larger, yes, and it was roughly the same size as a human head, but that was all. There were no eyes. No nose. No mouth. Just a large, rapidly growing patch of dark stuff on the roof.

"That does it."

My shift had been long and difficult. The combined exhaustion of work and the stress of that growing patch on the roof was getting to me. I slammed the apartment door behind me, stomped up the stairs, and knocked on the door of 804.

"Hello!"

I banged again.

"Hello! Is anyone in there?"

I banged a few more times and waited. This wasn't me. I wasn't the type of person to bang on neighbours' doors at night. But enough was enough. That stain was coming from somewhere, and if it was spreading that fast, then the apartment above had to be the culprit.

No response. I banged a few more times and stuck my face to the window. No lights or signs of life. Maybe they weren't home yet. I ran back downstairs, grabbed a pen and paper, quickly scribbled a note and ran back up. I taped it to the door.

"This is 704. There is a large water stain on my bedroom roof. Could you please check for any leaks or other water damage? Thank you."

That would do it. Simple and to the point.

"Ah, shit." As I reached the stairs landing to return to my own apartment, I realised I'd left some important work papers in the car. Exhaustion really was taking its toll on me. If I didn't get those filled out by tomorrow, the head nurse would rip me a new one. Again.

I pressed the button for the elevator. Nothing happened. I pressed again and again, growing angrier by the minute. Why was all this happening to me? Why couldn't something, anything, go my way for once?

"Fine!" I said to no-one in particular. I stomped down all eight flights of stairs, my will to live draining with each step. "Should just go back home... Gotta be less stressful jobs back there than this shithole. Why did I ever wanna live in the big city in the first place?"

I grabbed the papers from the car and then pressed the button for the elevator again. It wasn't on the first floor, and it wasn't on the top floor. Again, nothing happened. "Oh, come on!" Where the hell was it?

I stomped back upstairs. Once I hit the third floor, a jolt startled me. My heart raced in my chest and I blinked a few times to make sure I wasn't seeing things.

"Uh…" A young couple leaned against the balcony railings, drenched head to toe in… blood?

"Painting accident," the woman said. I nodded and kept walking, giving them another nervous glance before picking up the pace. Painting accident, my ass. I was a nurse. I worked with blood day in, day out, and the smell of it on them almost made me sick.

Maybe Mei was right? Maybe Higanbana Heights really was haunted?

…Nah.

Puffing, I threw my apartment door open and almost tumbled inside. I was too tired for this shit. Just wanted a nice, long, quiet…

"Oh, come on…"

The stain had grown larger. In the time it had taken me to go upstairs, go downstairs, then come back upstairs, the dark patch on my roof had almost doubled. Now it was gaining a body to go with its head. At least, that was what it looked like.

I snapped a picture and sent it to Erika. *"I'm not going crazy, am I? That is mould, right?"*

It didn't even take 30 seconds for her to reply. *"Get out of the house."*

"I'm not leaving the house over a dark patch on the roof, are you crazy?"

"Seriously, mould or not, that's not right."

"I know, but…"

"Leave. You can spend the night here."

"You live on the other side of town."

"At least my house is ghost-free."

"It's not a ghost!"

"Then what is it?"

"I don't know!"

That was the problem. I really had no idea.

"It has to be coming from upstairs. I'm gonna go up there and check again."

"Don't do that! You don't know who lives up there! They could be murderers!"

Why was everything a ghost or a murderer with her?

"I'll be back soon," I said and put the phone in my back pocket. Just in case.

Exhausted, I dragged myself upstairs again. I knocked on the door, ready to rest my forehead against it and/or collapse to the ground. Still no response. I banged again, this time harder. Something clicked, and the door popped open.

Uh…

"…Hello?" I spoke through the tiny gap that had opened. "Is anyone here? I'm from downstairs…"

Nothing. I pushed the door open a little further and recoiled in horror. "Oh god…" It stank. I knew that smell very well. The stench of death.

I fumbled for the light switch. It didn't work. No electricity. Huh. I grabbed my phone and turned the spotlight feature on. It didn't give much light, but it was better than nothing.

"Hello?" I called out again. I no longer expected a response, but just in case somebody was hiding, I didn't want to disturb them. "Is anyone here? I'm coming in! Hello?"

The apartment was a carbon copy of my own, only danker and smellier. I tried the kitchen light and still nothing. Judging by the state of the place, nobody had lived in it for quite some time, so the utilities had no doubt been cut. I tried the tap. No water.

No water…

A chill ran down my spine. A voice in the back of my head told me to get out. Get out and never return. Take Erika up on her offer and spend the night at her place. That patch wasn't mould, and I knew it. It was something else. Something else that I didn't want to discover, and if I kept poking my nose around where I shouldn't, then I soon would.

Yet I had to know. The stain was in my bedroom. I walked down the short hall. The bedroom door was closed. I coughed, the stench causing me to gag. I thought I was used to it, but maybe not. Or maybe this was something else.

"Hello?" I called out one last time and rapped on the door with my knuckles. Just in case. I waited, but there was no response. I reached for the handle, my heart pounding furiously in my chest, and swallowed. 'Here goes nothing.'

I flung the door open, taking a step back and readying myself. For what, I didn't know, but I froze and waited for something to tear through me. A ghost maybe, I didn't know. But there was no ghost. There was nothing supernatural at all.

"Oh god…"

I turned and puked on the floor. With shaking hands, I dialled 110.

* * *

"It was a dead body?"
I nodded.

"Oh god. Oh... eww. That's gross."

"They think that he'd been there for a while now, to reach that state of decay."

"That state of... oh I'm gonna be sick." Erika gagged and fought the urge to throw up in front of me. "So that stain was..."

"...His body liquefying above me."

"Yeah, I'm gonna be sick..."

She wasn't the only one. The more I thought about it, the more it creeped me out. It wasn't mould. It was... people juices. A man liquefying in the summer heat, his decaying liquids dripping through the floor and forming a puddle on my roof. Getting larger by the day as the heat rotted his body further and further. It was no ghost, but finally learning the truth, I almost wished it was.

"How can you still live in that place?" Erika came back, wiping her mouth and holding a glass of water.

"The body's gone now. They're gonna send someone out to fix the roof."

"That's not the point! Ugh, I could never stay in a place where a man had literally rotted above me and soaked into the roof. That's disgusting. Bits of it might have fallen down on you while you slept. You could have *swallowed* bits of his liquefied flesh as it dripped from the roof!"

"Well when you put it like that..."

It was disgusting, but Higanbana Heights was close to work and the rent was cheap. And about to get even cheaper, if the landlord was to be believed. A little something to keep me there after all the "pain and trauma" I had experienced. I wasn't blind.

APARTMENT 704

I'd seen the number of free apartments in the building rapidly rising over the years. People coming and going at all hours, and the building falling more and more into disrepair.

But moving was such a hassle, and if the price was right, well…

"You're crazy, you know."

"Maybe."

"You wanna get drinks after work tonight? My treat."

"Sounds great."

* * *

I lay in bed, looking up at the roof. The body had been gone several days, and they had painted over the dark spot until they could get someone in to replace that section of roof entirely. Everything was back to normal. Or at least, it should have been.

A face looked down at me where they had painted over the stain. Its mouth twisted in pain. Its eyes pleading. Dark tendrils spread out from it, twisting throughout the roof.

I closed my eyes. The body was gone. They cleaned everything up. There was nothing there now. It was just a body. Ghosts didn't exist.

Just a body.

"Pleaseeee…" The soft, pained words echoed throughout the quiet room.

I turned over and squeezed my eyes shut. It was just a body. Nothing more. I was just tired. That was all. They'd replace the roof soon. Everything would be fine.

Just a body…

APARTMENT 804

A SHARP WIND KICKED UP, and heavy rain pelted my face.

"Wonderful…"

The cardboard boxes that functioned as my shelter weren't going to be enough to keep that out, not even with the tarps over them. Several other men nearby took shelter under their own "hobo huts," as we liked to call them, but a quick glance told me all I needed to know. Nobody thought we'd make it out the end of this one intact.

Damn typhoons.

A few guys had already vacated. They recognised the signs coming in and moved to the nearby station to try their luck. They might get kicked out, sure, but with this kind of weather they might get lucky and the station master might turn a blind eye to them. Only one way to find out, right?

Why hadn't I gone with them? Ugh.

My worldly possessions were the clothes on my

back and a small bag of various odds and ends I had picked up along the way. An old discarded hairbrush, a bottle of water, a couple of tattered paperbacks, and a face towel. That would do me little good against the deluge that was threatening to wash both us and our hobo huts away.

What did I have to lose? Literally? Other than my life. I could cling to these cardboard boxes I called home, or I could head out into the rain before it got even worse and try to find somewhere, anywhere safer than this.

Would I lose my hut? Sure. Once the typhoon passed, some other guy would no doubt move in and claim my tiny piece of land. "You snooze, you lose." Then I could start a scene and try to reclaim my spot, getting into a hilarious fight that would no doubt amuse the other guys starved of entertainment.

But was it worth it? Was it worth risking my life to brave the night out in the open? Guys had died from less, and a heavy, wet leaflet smacked me in the face as the wind tossed things around.

Gross.

I pulled it from my face, pieces tearing off as it did, and sighed. I grabbed my bag, pulled my hood even closer around my neck, gave the man next to me a nod, and then ran. He nodded back, shivering against the rain and wind. He wouldn't give up his spot for anything. Only death would take it from him. Well, better him than me.

Wind roared all around. It whistled and hissed and as objects got thrown around, and it crashed and banged too. What a mess. I shivered, even in the summer heat, soaked through to the bone mere moments after leaving the safety of my tarp. The tarp that was already flapping wildly in the breeze, hard enough to give me whiplash if it decided to smack me in the face. If anyone wanted to steal that tonight, more power to them.

I passed by the station. Too many people taking shelter there already. Besides, the station master had it out for me ever since I broke in that time to get some drinks for my buddies. You see, what most people didn't know is that vending machines have a function that allows anyone to get drinks for free. Absolutely free.

It was something I'd picked up at my previous job. After the death of my startup, I ran some of the busiest vending machine lines in Tokyo to make ends meet. I was the guy they sent out to collect the cash, make sure machines stayed stocked, and also bug test anything not working as intended. All you needed was a single 100 yen coin and two 10 yen coins and you could have as many drinks as you wanted. The catch? You had to know the particular pattern.

Each machine had its own pattern, and if you knew it, 120 yen would get you as many drinks as you wanted. I'd worked the station vending machines before I got fired and they still hadn't changed the patterns. 10 yen coin, 100 yen coin, 10 yen coin. Pick a drink. Wait ten seconds. Press the refund button. Money comes back. Easy.

Only the station master caught me while I was at it and called the police. I couldn't go back there, not even tonight. Jail might be nicer than out here in the typhoon, but only for a single night.

I needed somewhere safe and quiet, just for the night. I'd be gone after that. Numerous high rises reached into the clouds above me. Yeah. Maybe one of those. Apartments all over the city were empty. I'd also learnt that from my startup. We installed optic fibre cables for high speed internet all around the city, and made a killing from it too. Until my business partner ran off with all the money *and* my wife. May they both rest in hell.

But the point was, a lot more apartments were empty than they appeared from the outside. The rent in the city was high, and people were constantly moving for work. There had to be at least one I could get into. Just for the night. Any longer than that brought with it the risk of nearby tenants finding out and police being called in. I didn't want either of those.

Higanbana Heights. A large building rose before me, its sign old and stained. Rain pelted my eyes, making it difficult to see, but the car park was, for the most part, empty.

Perfect.

Tree branches grabbed for my face as I ran for cover. Lights lit up the open space surrounding the letter boxes and elevator, highlighting the large amount of litter that had already blown in. The elevator would be quickest, but I couldn't risk any of the tenants seeing me.

The stairs it was.

The upper levels held the most likelihood of being empty, so I'd start from the top and work my way down. Any apartments that were clearly lived in I could avoid, and the others, well, a little door jiggling or window sneaking would have me inside in no time.

Something else I'd learnt during my fibre optic time, a scary amount of real estates in the big city simply left their unattended apartments unlocked. Supposedly to make it easy for the water, gas, and electricity guys to get in and out and do their thing, but I think most were just lazy and honestly didn't care.

Rain and wind pelted the stairs, howling through the tight spaces and making the climb both slippery and noisy. The higher I climbed, the worse it got. When I reached the top floor, I leaned against the wall and sighed. As I'd suspected, not a single person noticed me—because really, who wanted to come outside in this?—but you could never be too sure.

Four apartments spread out to the left of me, four to the right. Various pot plants decorated the doorstep of the apartment to my left, while very little decorated any of the apartments to my right. I tried the first door. Tiny, scratched, almost rusted silver letters on the door said 804. Eight floors? Damn. No wonder I was tired.

I peeked in through the window. Basic curtains covered it, but that meant nothing. No lights were on, nor could I hear anything over the increasing rage of the wind. I grabbed the door handle and braced myself. If it was locked, I'd slip by to the next apartment. If it opened, then bingo.

I turned the handle. It opened with a soft click.

Bingo.

I slipped in and pushed the door closed against the wind with a bang. Nobody would notice that, not in this weather. The aggressive roars of the wind turned to echoing howls around the wonderfully dry apartment and I smiled.

Peace. Quiet. Shelter.

I turned around and almost jumped out of my skin. "What the hell?" The words escaped my lips before I could stop them. Oh no. This was bad. This was really bad.

The place was fully furnished. A couch. TV. Table and fridge in the kitchen. Somebody *lived* here.

Adrenaline shot through me. Panic seized my mind. What if they were still here? What if they were asleep in bed and I'd just broken into their house with a nice loud bang and now they were standing around the corner with a large kitchen knife, or…?

I shook my head. An honest mistake. Nothing more. Sure, nobody liked being woken up by a drenched homeless guy dripping all over their living room floor, but these things happened. Mistakes were made. A simple apology and…

I stopped. A chill ran through me that wasn't the water seeping into my bones. I took a step, and then another. A dinner plate sat on the kitchen table. Spaghetti, or at least, what had once been spaghetti. Now it was a mould colony, and the husk of bread next to it didn't look any better. A tipped over glass lay on the table beside them. Whatever had been inside it had dried into a sticky substance.

"…Hello?" I didn't know what had taken a hold

of me, but something wasn't right here. Who left mouldy food on the table and their door unlocked?

"Hello?" I called out a little louder, but I still barely heard myself over the wind whipping up outside. I peered down the hall. Three doors, all closed. I waited, my breath catching in my throat. No signs of movement and no signs of life.

I turned back and opened the fridge. The light inside came on and a blast of cold washed over me. The electricity was still on, that was good to know. Also, it was full of food. Well, "full of" was maybe an exaggeration, but considering my last meal had been a half-eaten sandwich I'd dug out of a convenience store bin two days ago, this was a feast.

Before I could stop myself, I grabbed an apple, some pre-wrapped rice balls, and a bottle of tea. A glorious, magnificent feast. Once I would have turned my nose up at this. Once, in better times and with far more money, I would have scoffed at the idea of pre-wrapped rice balls. Now? I was shoving it down my throat before I even knew what I was doing. No time to savour when your stomach was on the verge of eating itself instead.

I tore the cap off the bottle of tea and washed the rice down with it. Ah, how long had it been since I'd had some good, honest barley tea? Too long. The light in the fridge suddenly went out and I jumped. A chill settled over me and I nervously smiled. I'd just left the door open for too long, that was all. I closed it and looked around the room again.

The mouldy bread seemed to stare at me, telling

a story I wasn't sure I wanted to hear. Turning the lights on would be a great way to get noticed, and that was the one thing I wanted to avoid most of all.

Shivers wracked my body. From the wet clothes or something else? I shook my head and peered around the corner again. All three doors were still closed. No angry owners rushing me for eating their food or sneaking into their apartment at night. It was empty. Whoever lived here had left in such a hurry they left their dinner on the table and the door open. They'd be back, no doubt... but probably not tonight. Not in this weather.

I smiled. Tonight, this was my apartment, and I was going to enjoy it as such.

I discarded my dirty clothes on the bathroom floor and turned the tap. After a few moments hot water came steaming out and I almost collapsed into a puddle on the spot. Hot. Water. Truly, how long had it been? I jumped under it in the darkness and let it soak into my chilled skin. My sigh of relief was audible even with the howling wind.

Something crashed outside. I jumped, freezing under the water and letting it wash over me as I listened. Was the owner home? Were they about to find me naked and taking a shower in their bathroom? This was about to very awkward, if so.

Wind continued to beat against the window. Warm water slowly sucked the chill from my bones, yet not from my heart.

Footsteps. No doubt about it. Like heavy boots coming down the hall. They stopped right in front of the door. Instinctively, I covered my privates with my hands, yet I still could not otherwise move.

I could explain. With the typhoon outside I just needed a place to spend the night, and the door was unlocked, and…

The handle jiggled. Oh god. My pile of wet clothes lay in the middle of the room. Between me and whoever was on the other side of that door. If I could reach them before the door opened, I could toss them in the person's face and make a run for it. I'd be without clothes, but I'd be alive. I'd take that.

I took a step out from beneath the water, and then another. One more would have me close enough to grab the wet rags and ready myself.

The handle jiggled again. I reached for the clothes.

Another jiggle. I tightened my grip.

Silence. Water beat softly on the tiles behind me, almost drowned out by the rain hitting the tiny bathroom window. I pulled the wet clothes towards me, inch by inch, until I was in the perfect position to throw them. Right in the face. Create enough surprise and enough of an impact to push my way through. A towel hung from the rack nearby. I could grab it on my way past to protect my modesty.

Holding my breath, I waited. And waited. And waited some more. My muscles started to seize from the effort of holding the heavy pile of wet rags at the ready, crouched low on the ground to leap and push the man off guard.

All the lights in the house were off. I couldn't see any shadow on the other side of the door. I couldn't see anything. Just darkness and vague shapes within it.

A minute passed. My muscles were too weak. I

couldn't keep this up any longer. I stood up, slowly, my muscles screaming in pain, and dragged the clothes to the door. I reached for the handle with my left hand while I held the clothes ready in my right.

'Here goes,' I thought. 'On three. One… Two…'

I pushed the handle down and yanked it, screaming as I threw the pile of wet rags I called clothes. They hit the opposing door and fell to the ground with a wet thud.

Nobody was there.

I stuck my head out the door. The other two doors were closed, and the rest of the apartment looked exactly the same as when I'd entered.

"Geez, getting jumpy in my old age," I muttered. I turned around and screamed.

A face appeared right in front of me in the darkness of the room. Not my own face in the mirror, oh no. A dark face, the skin ashy, blood running from the man's eyes and ears. His eyes, dark and sunken in like black holes, lolled aimlessly around the room until fixing upon me, and then he moved.

Would anyone hear my screams in the typhoon? It was a strange thought to have, perhaps, but the only conscious thought that crossed my mind as pure terror took over and I ran back down the hall, dropping the towel and forgetting all about my modesty.

I grabbed the first thing I could from the table—the knocked over cup—and threw it down the hall. The empty hall. It landed on the ground with a dull thud near my clothes. I grabbed the mouldy bread and threw that too. Just in case.

The man didn't follow. I stood behind the table, chest rising and falling rapidly as I tried to calm my breath, and once again a slight chill settled into my skin. From the water clinging to me or from what I'd just seen, who knew. Perhaps both.

I shouldn't have come here. I should have stayed in my little cardboard shack down in the park where the police left me alone and the occasional jogger dropped a note for me to buy some breakfast. It was only a single night. I'd experienced worse than this. Why did I pick this apartment of all places to shelter from the storm? It didn't even make any sense. The damn thing must have called me here, luring me into its belly so it could devour me.

Well, not this guy. I'd been through worse than this in my life. If I could survive the loss of my business, the loss of my wife and best friend, the loss of the child that may or may not have been mine to begin with, the loss of literally everything I owned, I could survive this. No damned ghost was going to—

"Ahh!!" My screams tore through the apartment once more as the face suddenly appeared right next to me. No footsteps. No sounds to herald its arrival. It was just there, as though it had warped in. I tossed the plate with the mouldy spaghetti at it and ran back down the hall. By the time I came to regret that decision, it was already too late. I should have run for the front door, not further into the belly of the beast... Moron...

I jumped over the wet pile of clothes and reached for the door handle. The door flung open with a bang, colliding with the wall hard enough to leave a small dent where the handle was. A single futon lay spread out in the middle of the room with a tiny bedside stand next to it.

Nowhere to hide. Nowhere to go.

The door slammed shut. I screamed again, almost jumping out of my skin. I ran for it, jiggling the handle as hard as I could. It refused to budge.

"No, no, no! Come on! Open up! I'm sorry! I didn't mean to intrude! I'll leave! Just let me go!" The words came out of their own volition. Terror coursed through me, blinding my vision as I tunnelled in on the handle, the one thing keeping me from freedom. Or so my fear-addled brain told me.

"Help me," a voice whispered by my ear, far too close for comfort. I screamed again, spinning around, but the room was empty.

"Come on, come on!" I jiggled the handle again, unable to tear my eyes from the room, when again I heard it in the other ear.

"Help me."

I ran for the bedroom window, flicking the switch keeping it closed and sliding it open before I could stop myself. Rain pelted me in the face, and a quick look outside soon reminded me where I was. Eight floors up and no balcony to escape onto. Just a nice eight-story drop and my painful, bloody death below.

The closet doors rattled and threatened to come flying off. They were traditional sliding doors with a generic picture painted in the bottom corner to give the illusion of Japanese aesthetics, but everyone knew they were just cheap trash.

"Stop!" I screamed. Rain and wind continued to

pelt me from the open window as the sliding doors shook. "I'm sorry! Just let me go! I'll never come back again!"

They shook more violently, and I ran over to brace them. One knock to the head from a flying door would no doubt be enough to do me in. Although at this rate, maybe that would be preferable. What else awaited me? A night in a small, dingy apartment with a ghost hunting me and a typhoon raging outside? Maybe death by sliding door to the head was actually preferable to whatever the ghost had in store for me.

"Help me…" That voice again, this time directly behind my head. I closed my eyes and continued pushing against the rocking doors. He was there. I knew it. If I opened my eyes and turned around, that face would be right there, blood pouring from his eyes and ears, the sunken hollows of his face staring into my soul. Devouring me from the inside. Stealing my soul…

The rocking stopped. Everything stopped. It was like, for the briefest of moments, we had entered the eye of the typhoon. That didn't even make any sense. It didn't happen like that. Not so fast that everything suddenly stopped at once. No, this was like time itself froze. Only it hadn't, because the moment I turned back to the window, rain started pouring in again. Wind whipped up a frenzy. Puddles formed on the floor beneath it.

Yet the sliding doors stopped. No more rocking and jerking. They were regular doors once more.

'Open them,' a voice inside my head told me. 'Climb in there. Hide from the rain. Hide from the spirit. Hide from the evil lurking in the very walls, threatening to consume you. It won't get you in there. Hide. Flee. Be safe.'

My hand trembled against the small dip that was the handle. All I had to do was slide my hand across and the door would open. I could crawl into the closet, close it behind me, and sink into the safety and warmth of the enclosed four walls. Nothing could sneak up on me. The rain couldn't get me.

Safety. Warm, dry safety.

My hands moved of their own accord, the door sliding ever so slowly across the tracks. My heart pounded wildly. Why wouldn't it open faster? Why couldn't I move? I wasn't the one doing this. I was, but I wasn't. The conscious part of me wanted to run. The unconscious part of me was already opening the door.

The door stopped in its tracks with a soft bang, fully opened.

I opened my mouth to scream, but no sound came out.

A body, rotten and decaying, sat curled in the foetal position in the closet. Its dark, sunken eyes stared directly at me, blood running down its cheeks. Similar streams poured from its ears. Its lips pulled back in a horrifying grin, baring its teeth like a dog ready to attack.

I wanted to scream, but no sound came out.

"Help me!" The roar filled the room, sending tingles throughout my entire body as the corpse leapt forward and wrapped its bony fingers around my neck. I struggled, but I was no match. Water pounded my skin from the violent rain outside and I gasped for air, feebly grabbing at the inhumanly strong wrists squeezing my throat. Soon there would be a crack. I could feel it coming.

So this was it. 10 years on the streets were about to come to an end in an unknown apartment in a typhoon. I would die naked, alone, drenched in water in an apartment with an already dead body in the closet. A dead body bringing me into its world. Would we be trapped together? Roommates for eternity in the afterlife until someone else discovered us? How did that work, anyway? And why was the thought crossing my mind now of all times?

The demon's eyes turned red, the sunken hollows growing even blacker as my vision faded.

Would anyone remember me? Did the boy I called a son even know who I was, or had they erased me from his life too? No. I would die another nameless face. Just another homeless guy poking around where he shouldn't have been. A terrible tragedy that nobody would miss.

Other dark figures emerged from the corners of the room, watching over us. Ah. He wasn't even the first. Perhaps he wouldn't be the last, either.

Ah.

I should have stayed in the safety of my cardboard in the park.

Now I was one of them.

Trapped.

Forever.

APARTMENT 201

THREE MONTHS HAD PASSED SINCE my son's death. His father was never around to begin with, and I had nothing left back home, so I made the decision to move to Tokyo. Start anew. Get my train wreck of a life back on track. That was the goal, anyway. Things never truly go as planned.

There was a lot they didn't tell you about the death of a child. How hard it was to deal with all the cold, methodical paperwork, the bored officials who'd seen it all and would see it again, the funeral industry trying to fleece you for all you have during your moment of grief... And perhaps the most painful act of all; clearing out your child's things.

To make the move to Tokyo, I downgraded a lot. Took only the essentials. Some clothes, some memorabilia, a few beloved ornaments and decorations I'd picked up over the years. But cleaning out Haruki's room had been the hardest of all.

Technically, I didn't need any of it. What was I going to do with a toy train? A box of action figures? I certainly didn't need five books on how to count and how to start reading basic Japanese. I had few friends, and none with small children who could benefit from them. It felt wrong to throw them away, but it also felt wrong to sell them. I couldn't keep them, but I couldn't get rid of them. Nobody told you about things like that.

In the end, I compromised. I kept a single box of Haruki's most beloved toys. Everything else I donated. No money exchanged hands and nothing got trashed. Haruki would have wanted it that way.

I rubbed my eye a little harder than intended, a tiny flame of rage flaring up inside. Now was not the time for crying. I'd done my fair share and then some. I placed the box in the spare room along with the rest of the unpacked items and closed the door. Out of sight, out of mind, they said.

They were stupid.

* * *

"I'm home," I said to no-one in particular, dragging my feet through the door. It was a habit I'd yet to break, and it gave me a sense of comfort. A tiny bit of normalcy in a world that was anything but normal. What world tore a child from his mother's arms and then continued on as though nothing had happened?

I dumped the convenience store bag with my dinner on the table and fell onto the couch. The sun would be rising in a few hours. Would this be considered dinner or breakfast? Night shift wasn't the worst thing in the world, and even in the big city the convenience stores were still mostly empty at night, making the job easy enough. Mindless, but sometimes that was nice.

Something in the hall caught my eye. I sat up and looked closer. "What the...?"

Haruki's favourite little blue train. I tilted my head and got off the couch to pick it up. "What on earth is that doing here?"

The door to the spare room was closed. All the doors were closed. I hadn't been in the spare room for days, and I certainly hadn't had any guests over. So... how? I reached for the handle and froze for a moment. What if someone was inside? What if this was a trap? Luring me into the spare room where they could then assault me.

It didn't make sense, but neither did this train lying in the hall. How else could you explain it? Someone had placed it there. Deliberately. A lure, and I was walking right into it.

Jumbled thoughts rushed through my mind, too fast to make sense of any of them. Go in? Don't go in? Call the police? Run fleeing in terror? If I called the police over finding a train in the hall, they'd laugh me out of my own house, and yet, if I didn't call them and someone was inside the room, waiting for me...

I flung the door open before I could stop myself.

The room was empty.

"Geez... Don't scare me like that." My heart pounded like a jackhammer in my chest, and pressure pushed against my temples. Oh good, another headache incoming. Just what I needed.

The box with Haruki's toys sat in the corner of the room where I'd left it, the top closed. I put the train back in and put another box on top of it. Just in case. There.

I dragged my feet back to the couch and grabbed the soon to expire rice ball that was dinner. Or breakfast. Whatever. It was cold and a little soggy, and at this hour of the night... morning... whatever, there were few channels even on the air. White noise after white noise blasted from the TV's tiny speakers. I turned it off and ate in silence.

So this was my life now, huh? Fitting. With Haruki gone, what light was there left in the world, anyway?

* * *

"Toyama-san, we need to get these crates on the shelf before the breakfast rush, okay?"

"Yes, sir."

"Don't forget to restock the drinks too, okay?"

"Yes, sir."

"Sotaro should be in soon for the morning shift, so make sure it's done before then, okay?"

"Yes, sir."

"Alright. I'll be out the back if you need anything."

"Yes, sir."

No, he wouldn't. Well, he would be there, but not if I needed anything. He'd be sleeping. Yamada wasn't my boss, not technically, but he'd worked at the store longer than me and so had seniority. Shelf stacking was below him, even though we—again, technically—had the same job.

He disappeared out the back and I pushed the trolley of various breads and pastries over. Not a single customer in the entire store. In fact, there hadn't been one for the last hour or so. Fine for me, probably not so fine for the business. Whatever. That was their problem to worry about, not mine.

I placed the bags of melon bread on the empty shelves and another pang tore through me. Haruki's favourite. He especially liked the ones with the slightly crispy outside coated in sugar and a dab of melon-flavoured cream in the middle. I liked the smooth ones myself, the ones where more than half of the inside was intensely flavoured cream and the top was coated in something like a thin melon-flavoured cookie. We used to eat them together by the park near our house. The bakery down the road always sold them to us fresh, and sometimes he even gave Haruki a lollipop on the side.

Sighing, I tossed the rest of the bags on the shelf and moved onto the sandwiches. I had to stop this. Haruki was gone. He didn't exist anymore. Bringing these memories up all the time would do me no good. I moved here for a fresh start. It was what Haruki would have wanted as well. My sweet, adorable little boy...

"I said, excuse me."

I jumped. A man stood by the register with several cans of sake on the counter, and his eyebrows raised. "Can I get some service or what?"

"I'm terribly sorry." I rushed behind the counter and started ringing up the man's items. I hadn't even noticed he was there, I was so caught up in my own world. See, this was exactly why I had to stop. Moving on wasn't forgetting his memory. It was honouring his memory. Getting fired from the only job I'd been able to find on such short notice and ending up homeless wouldn't be what Haruki wanted. I had to do better.

So why was it so hard?

* * *

"You've gotta be kidding me."

Haruki's toy train lay in the hall, and it wasn't the only thing. This time it was joined by a car, several crayons, and a smattering of scribbles on the bottom of the wall.

"What the hell?"

The door had most definitely been locked when I left. The veranda could probably be reached with a ladder, I guessed, but the kitchen door was locked as well. Nothing else in the house had been touched, and yet, Haruki's toys lay in the hall.

I opened the spare room door. The box on top of Haruki's toys had fallen over, but the top remained closed. I lifted the cardboard flaps. Everything inside looked just as it did when I placed the toys inside. Except for the fact that several were missing and now lying in the hall.

What on earth was going on?

On edge, I put the toys back and grabbed some tape from the kitchen. I sealed the box and then placed several more on top of it. Now the only way in would be getting through several layers of tape and other boxes. I returned to the kitchen and grabbed a wet rag. Pretty sure my rent didn't cover drawing all over the walls.

I rubbed and rubbed, but the crayon refused to budge. I scrubbed more frantically, but nothing. If anything it just seemed to be smudging the crayon further in. The stains spread and tears welled in my eyes.

"God dammit!" I collapsed to the floor and held my head in my hands. Who was doing this? And why? Who would torment the mother of a deceased child like this? I tossed the rag to the ground and closed my eyes, waiting for the world to stop spinning.

Haruki. It had to be Haruki. As stupid as it sounded, there was no other explanation. Part of him lingered or was attached to his stuff. What else could it be? He came here with me, following his favourite toys, and while I was gone, he was amusing himself in our new apartment.

A chill fell over me. My throat felt dry as a desert and I struggled to swallow the fear back down. I reached for the spare room handle and pushed it open a smidgen.

"...Haruki?" The moment I said it I felt stupid, but I had to check. Was my baby boy really still here with me? "Haruki? Baby? Is that you?"

No response. Nothing but cold, barren silence. A tear rolled down my cheek, and I pulled myself to my feet. What an idiot. Of course he wasn't here. Why would he be? Grief did crazy things to one's mind. As much as I wanted my baby boy back, he was gone, and I was alone.

All alone.

* * *

"Hey, hey, Toyoma, focus!"

"Huh? Oh, sorry."

Yamada clicked his fingers in front of my face. "What has gotten into you?"

"Nothing. I'm good. What were you saying?"

I was anything but good, but I couldn't let him know that. He'd take any opportunity to blab to the boss. He hadn't been subtle in his distaste for me. I think he was hoping someone younger and hotter would join him for the night shift. Instead, he got… me. A woman in her late 20s grieving for her lost child. Over the hill and completely undesirable in his eyes. Not that he could talk, being in his mid-30s with a stomach to make a sumo wrestler proud.

"I was saying, you really gotta clean the *oden* pot out. People around here really enjoy it for breakfast. Yeah, I dunno why either, but anyway, they do. Which means it's up to us to clean it thoroughly before the morning shift so we don't get any more complaints about funky taste. You hearing me now?"

By "we" he meant "me," but I nodded and kept my mouth shut.

"And are you sure you're okay? Your eyes are red. Are you even getting any sleep?"

No, I wasn't. Not really. Sleeping during the day was already hard enough, but it was punctuated by dreams of Haruki running up and down the hall, laughing and playing, and constantly waking up to find that no, he wasn't there. Nothing was there. Not even his toys. It was all in my head. Nothing more.

"Listen, whatever's going on, deal with it. Get some light-killing curtains or something. You're here to do the night shift. That comes with certain drawbacks and benefits, but if you can't do your job, well…"

Was he really threatening me? Now? I forced the best smile I could and shook my head. "I'm fine. I'll clean the oden."

"Good. And make it snappy. Tomorrow's shipment of bread just came in and that needs to be put out before the morning shift as well."

Of course it did.

"I'll be out the back doing some administrative stuff, okay. If there's any trouble—"

"I know. I'll be fine. Thank you."

He eyed me for a moment before turning and silently returning to the back room. I sighed. Finally, he was gone.

A figure in the curved mirror on the roof caught my eye. I spun around, but nobody else was in the store. This time in the other mirror. A child, judging by the size. I looked through each of the aisles.

"Hello?"

I checked the mirrors again. Nothing. I returned to the oden and pulled the plug. Maybe he was right. Maybe night shift was getting to me and I should invest in some better curtains and maybe some earplugs or something.

Something giggled down the end of the aisle. I spun around. Nothing there. The store was empty. I slapped my cheek a few times, shook my head, and started removing the contents of the oden into bowls to clean the machine.

A bag of chips hit the floor. I turned around again. At least, that was what it sounded like. I searched the aisles, but there was nothing amiss. No bags on the floor. Nothing. Just an empty store and a tired woman running around like a madman.

"Oh my god, get it together." I turned around and nearly screamed. The man before me jumped in return.

"Ah!"

"Ah!"

"Sorry… I just wanted to get some…" He held up a bag of chips and some gum. How had I missed him? A loud noise buzzed whenever a customer entered the store, loud enough that you could hear it from out the back. Maybe it was on the fritz? I smiled and apologised and rang up the man's items. As he stepped back out through the automatic doors, they buzzed.

…Huh.

Maybe I *was* going mad. That would explain a lot.

* * *

I stood at the head of the hallway, frozen. A toy train. A toy truck. Numerous crayons. And this time, Haruki's favourite action figure, Super Rider. I dropped the bag holding my dinner to the ground. A rice ball tumbled out and rolled over to the train.

"What in the…" I had no words. I triple checked

all the windows and locks before I went to work. I taped the box in the spare room and covered it in several other heavy boxes. I scrubbed what I could of the crayons off the wall. And yet now... there was more. Pictures scrawled halfway up the wall, crayons scattered all over the ground, some snapped and some with their paper casings torn off. And the toys... they were everywhere.

I ran straight to the kitchen door. Locked. I jiggled the kitchen window. Shut tight. I stepped over the toys and checked the bathroom. Too small for a human to fit through, but still locked and shut anyway. My bedroom, same. The window in the spare room led to the front veranda, which was the only place someone could possibly get through. It looked shut from the outside, but...

I braced myself and grabbed the handle. Here goes nothing.

Swinging the door open, I stepped inside as though to surprise whoever might have been hiding. The room was, of course, empty. Several boxes lay toppled on the floor and the tape ripped off Haruki's things. I grabbed the window and pulled. Shut tight.

"Seriously?"

A cold breeze blew over me and I turned around. Nothing. Nothing but an empty hall and toys lying everywhere.

The house was shut tight. How could there even be a breeze to begin with?

Something was wrong with this place. Something bad. Just being inside it made my skin crawl. This wasn't grief. It wasn't hoping that my baby boy had come back. This place was *wrong*.

If I let myself imagine for just a moment that this truly was Haruki's doing… why was he doing it? What could he be trying to tell me? How could I even be sure that it was him and not some evil manifestation created by this cheap, rundown apartment? I wasn't one to believe in the supernatural, but I wasn't stupid either. Something was going on here, and I could find no rational explanation for it.

The apartment was haunted.

That, or I had the world's smartest troublemaker with a personal vendetta against me. Both sounded stupid in my head, but as I looked at the toys and the pictures scrawled all over the walls, what other explanation was there? If it happened while I was awake then maybe I could explain it away as sleepwalking. But it happened when I wasn't here. Someone, or something, was doing this to taunt me.

Why? That was the million dollar question.

I picked the toys up and placed them back in the box. I didn't bother taping it again. Why bother? It would just get ripped off again anyway. Whatever was going on, a little tape wasn't going to stop it. Maybe if I moved it? There wasn't really anywhere in the apartment to hide something though. Under the couch? I didn't feel comfortable sitting on top of that, and it felt like hiding Haruki's memory. He deserved better than that.

I sighed, grabbing the washcloth from the sink and scrubbing the walls again. It did nothing. I fell down to the ground and lay my head back against the wall. At times like this Haruki would run over, place a tiny hand on my head and ask, "What's wrong, Mama?" "I'm just tired, baby." "You should rest, Mama." "I know, but I'm so busy." "I can do it. I'm a big boy now." And he'd smile and pat my head, imitating what I'd done to him so many times over his young life, and my heart would melt.

A tear escaped my eye. It was too much. All of this was too much. No child deserved to die so young, let alone my beautiful baby boy. As I stared at the crayons staining the wall, the thought briefly crossing my mind how much this would cost to fix, I noticed something. Another chill settled over me.

Words mixed in with the scribbling. Hiragana, written in a child's hand. *"Help." "Please." "Why?"*

Swallowing, I pushed myself up the wall, unable to stop the trembling of my knees. Haruki. It had to be. But why? What did it mean? Help? Please? Why? What was he trying to tell me? Was he lost and confused because of the move? Had the painful nature of his death caused him to get stuck here, unable to move on? But why hadn't he made himself known to me sooner? Three months had passed. More than enough time if he really was here and had something he needed to say.

"…Haruki?" It hurt to say that name and not have him come running with a big smile on his face. "Haruki, baby, are you here?" How stupid I must have looked, standing in a hallway calling to a dead child. But if it was him, I had to make sure. I had to help him. I was the only family he had.

"Baby? If you're here, let Mummy know, okay?" Crayons lay sprawled on the ground where he… where someone had left them. I stared at them, waiting for one to move. Nothing. Yet I shivered. The house felt far too cold for the summer heat, even at this early hour of the morning. The sun would be up soon, but in Tokyo, the heat didn't die when it went down. It simmered under the surface, coating everything, choking everything, lying in wait to roar to life once more as a new day began.

So why couldn't I stop shivering?

"Help." "Please." I searched through the mass of red, black, and yellow on the wall. Placing a hand on the words, I traced over the crayon, as though searching through a map. There had to be something here. There had to be. Why else was it here? Haruki loved drawing. This was his way of telling me something. It was in there somewhere.

There.

I stepped back to get a better view overall. An arrow pointing up. I followed it to the ceiling, but there was nothing there. Another arrow, this one under a swirling rage of red. Also pointing up. Another, this time under a black house that had been violently filled in with red. All of them pointed up.

The ceiling.

I ran to the living room, my eyes glued to the roof. There had to be a way up there somehow. Workers had to get in there to fix things. My previous house had a covering in the bathroom. It always weirded me out, thinking someone might be hiding up there as I washed.

Nothing in the living room. Nothing in the kitchen. I ran to the bathroom. Nothing there either. It wasn't in the spare room. That just left... my room.

Flinging the door open, I ran inside, eyes glued above me. Nothing. No covering to get into the crawlspace.

"Dammit!"

My eyes fell on the closet. Of course! I flung the door open and fell back in horror.

Arrows. Thousands of them, all pointing to the covering in the corner of the roof. Violent swirls and angry scribbles covered every square inch of the closet walls. All of them black and red.

My heart pounded in my chest. The only thing I could hear was the beating of my heart in my ears as adrenaline coursed through me.

"Haruki?" The word escaped my lips as a mere whisper. Bracing myself, I climbed into the closet. Cold. So cold. Shivering, I pushed up on the covering and tossed it aside. An avalanche of dust poured down, sending me into a coughing fit. Ugh, when was the last time anyone came up here?

I stuck my head in. Pitch black. I grabbed the phone from my pocket and pressed the button, casting a soft light over the area. Beams, pipes, some wires, and... there.

I couldn't stop the racing of my heart. Pushing against the walls of the closet with my feet, I climbed into the crawlspace and ignored the cobwebs blocking my way.

"Haruki!" The echo of my own voice boomed all around me. Why was it so cold?

I grabbed the tiny mass lying in the middle of the roof. Right above the arrows in the hall. Pointing me here. Leading me to this discovery.

"Haruki, is that—" The words died on my lips. It wasn't Haruki. It wasn't my baby boy at all. Why would it be? Haruki hadn't died here. Haruki didn't know this place at all.

A skeleton lay face down on the roof, a dirty dress draped over the bones. It had to be a girl of no more than four or five, judging by the size of her. I shone the phone light around the tiny body and fought back the scream of terror threatening to escape from my lips.

Crayons. A different brand to Haruki's. Older. Much older. Most had been worn down to nearly nothing, and for good reason. The entire roof was covered in scribbles. The tiny bones of the girl's hand still clutched a crayon in her hand. A red crayon. Beneath it, beneath her, lay the girl's dying words.

"Mama. Help me. Please. Why? I'm sorry. Mama. Help me. Please. Why? I'm sorry."

Something behind me banged. I spun around, the light from my phone shining on a dark, bony hand as it pulled the crawlspace covering back into place.

"No!" The word echoed painfully again.

"…Mama?"

I spun back. The skeleton turned to look at me through empty, cavernous eyes.

"Mama!"

My phone clattered to the floor. Cold, bony fingers tightened around my neck.

It wasn't Haruki. Haruki was gone, long moved on to a better place. Of course he had. What a fool I was. I closed my eyes.

"Mama." The voice grew deep. Gravelly. Right

by my ear.

An odd calm washed over me. Soon we'd be together again.

Soon.

APARTMENT 503

Third time's the charm, right? After two failures of trying to get into my university of choice, this next time had to be it. My parents would only continue to support my efforts for so long, and heading into my third year of study so I could get into the best medical school in the country was already pushing their limits.

"Why medical school?" my father asked after I failed for the second time. "You can come and work for my company. I told you, a position's always open." Thanks, Dad, but even after telling him numerous times that stock trading wasn't for me, he still wouldn't let go of it.

Doctors actually helped people. Society needed them. They were respected, they made good money, and there was something about having "Dr." attached to your name that made people treat you differently. Treat you better.

Third time's the charm. Plus, it would get me out

of this crappy apartment, finally. Not to sound ungrateful, because I was anything but that, but everyone knew this place was a little… shady. People coming and going at all hours of the night. Screams in the early hours that woke all nearby. Police cordoning off rooms for weeks at a time while they investigated yet another murder or death. If I had any say in it, I'd be anywhere else but here. But I didn't. My parents paid the rent, and without work I could hardly argue.

Even more reason to pass the test, become a doctor, and get the hell outta here.

White noise flickered on the TV. Damn. It was that late already? I fumbled around in the dark for the remote. No job and no place to be meant I could keep my own hours, and nights suited me just fine. The city was, for the most part, quieter then. Although that silence meant I could hear the comings and goings outside my apartment all the more clearly.

"Ah, there you are." The remote lay on the floor beneath the TV. I reached down to grab it and a spot of light on the wall behind the TV stand caught my attention. "What the hell?"

I pushed the stand aside and frowned. A hole about two centimetres wide shone brightly behind it. When the hell did that happen? I knelt down and pressed my face to it.

"Holy shit…"

I could see into the neighbour's apartment, clear as day. The lights were still on, although I couldn't see or hear anybody. The layout was exactly the same as mine, right down to the placement of the

TV. If I so wanted, I could kick back and watch his instead of my own.

Suddenly the front door opened and a man entered, slamming it shut behind him. I jumped and scuttled away from the hole. I'd never directly introduced myself to my neighbour, but I'd seen him in passing. Long hair, grungy clothes. Looked like a musician or hippy artist type. Permanent scowl on his face. To be honest, I was too scared to introduce myself to him. I had no reason to be. Just a feeling. Yeah, my feelings weren't always right, but sometimes they were. I'd rather trust my gut instinct than not. You only had to be wrong once.

I stared at the TV stand for a moment. If I slid it back, it would cover the hole again. He'd have no idea I could see in. But that would also make a loud noise and draw his attention to it. My lights were off. He didn't know I was there. He no doubt had no idea the hole itself was there either. I should probably call the landlord about that… although the last time I called them to fix the leaking pipes it took them three weeks to send someone out.

Ah, whatever. Study had left me tired. First bed. Worry about the hole later.

* * *

The hole drew me in. I couldn't stop looking. When I wasn't in front of it, it consumed my thoughts. Study fell to the wayside because who needed that when I could stare through the hole? Sometimes I watched for hours when he wasn't even home. Watching. Waiting.

I saw a mouse run across the living room once. Another time a cockroach crawled right past the hole and scared the living daylights out of me. I was tempted to stick my finger through and see if I could reach it, but then I remembered how gross cockroaches were and nixed that idea.

Why was the hole so fascinating to me? Hours passed before I knew it and when I thought back, all I could remember was... an unchanging room. A blank TV on a nondescript stand. A small coffee table in the middle. A single armchair to the right and a stack of boxes to the left. I'd yet to figure out what was in the boxes, but it was likely where the mice and cockroaches were coming from. Maybe it was trash? Maybe it was people? My mind ran wild with possibilities. What could he be hiding in there, and why was he always coming and going at strange hours of the night?

He appeared to keep a schedule not too different to my own with one small difference; I didn't leave the house very much. I had no reason to. My parents gave me only a small allowance, and I spent most of that on cheap convenience store booze that I drank at home alone. No money to go out, no money to do nice things, and no friends because they were all around the country attending universities they'd actually gotten into. But this guy, he seemed to sleep during the day and then all night he was coming and going, talking to people on the phone, running out on errands, pacing the living room floor.

Maybe he was a drug dealer. No, no! A vampire! I smiled at the ridiculous idea. If he was a vampire, what did that make me? At least he went outside.

But what if…?

Nah.

The door slammed, and the man walked back inside. He screamed at someone on the other end of the phone and then hung up, tossing it onto the couch. He stormed past, rustled through one of the boxes, and then disappeared into the kitchen. What on earth was he doing? There was a loud bang, followed by another. I withdrew from the hole. No, those weren't gunshots. I had no idea what gunshots sounded like, but that couldn't have been it. There was no flash of light, no echo in my ear, nothing. He just punched the table or the wall or something.

As much as I wanted to hang around, that was enough peeping for one night. I didn't want him to catch me while he was clearly in a mood over something. That would not end well for anybody.

* * *

In an attempt to focus on my study again, I pushed the TV stand back over the hole. It almost worked. I threw myself into my books, writing notes and even making notations for those notes in different colours like I'd seen the girls do back in high school. I mean, they were in university now so there had to be something to it, right?

Yet my neighbour wouldn't shut the hell up. Night after night, banging and screaming. It sounded like he was demolishing the place, and my attempts at ignoring him were getting nowhere.

Another bang. I jumped in my chair and closed

my eyes. Just complain to the landlord. Let them deal with him. You have study to focus on. Forget the hole. Only a few more months until the tests that will decide the rest of your life. This is it. Not the hole. The hole has nothing to do with you. No matter how fascinating it is. How interesting it is. How it calls to you…

I jumped again. Another bang, louder this time. I looked down and noticed I'd drawn several violent circles all over my notes. "Alright, that's it!"

I was storming out the door before I could stop myself. Something had taken control of my body and before I knew what was happening, I banged on the man's door. "Hey! Hey!" It was 2 a.m. Not that it really mattered to him, and I was too angry to care if it woke anyone else up. How could they be sleeping through this noise anyway? He was incessant!

A few moments later the door flung open. "What?"

The fire in my veins that had pushed me out the door suddenly doused and my throat felt dry. "I, uh, I'm from next door…"

"…And?" He was even scarier up close. Perhaps not a vampire—he didn't seem to have any sharp fangs protruding from behind red lips—but it was hard to rule out some other type of violent criminal.

"…And I noticed you've been, uh, a little noisier than usual lately. I'm trying to study, and—" The door slammed in my face. Huh. Well, that went well. He didn't kill me.

I shuffled back to my apartment and softly closed the door behind me. I waited a moment, listening, before locking it and sliding the door chain across. I flicked the lock on the window facing the balcony as well. Just in case. Sure, if he wanted in then some window glass likely wouldn't stop him, but why make things easier, you know?

I fell on the couch and stared at the blank TV screen. The hole was just behind it. What was he doing right now? Was he plotting revenge? Planning my murder in excruciating detail? First, tear him limb from limb. Then plop his Daruma-like body into a cage and sell tickets on the black market for all to enjoy. Come see the amazing Daruma Man! Then, when I was no longer of any use, dump me in a river, unable to swim or move or do anything other than slowly, painfully drown like an anti-fish.

I shuddered. There was one way to check. Slide the TV stand across. Check the hole. Just a quick peep. My notes would still be there. If he was plotting revenge against me, however, I wouldn't. As crazy as the words sounded in my head, they still made perfect sense to me. Yes. Check the hole. Only way to find out.

I pressed my ear to the wall, listening. For once, the apartment was silent. I braced my shoulder against the TV stand and pushed. Slowly. Inch by inch. Careful not to make a single sound until the hole presented itself to me. Relief and endorphins flooded my body. Ah. There she was. Still waiting for me. Safe, welcoming, and unchanging. A constant in my inconstant world.

Well then, what was he up to? I pressed my eye to the hole. Hmm. The lights were off. Huh. Maybe my request had actually gotten through to him? Maybe he wasn't such a bad guy after all. I snorted before I could stop myself. All of that worry for nothing.

The guy was probably nothing more than a musician down on his luck, and those boxes were full of CDs he'd been unable to sell. Yeah. All of that yelling was him dealing with agents and venues, but musicians were a dime a dozen in Tokyo and getting a gig had to be hard. Had to be stressful. I created a life for this stranger who until moments ago I hadn't even seen up close and suddenly it all made sense.

The poor guy. After realising that someone actually lived next door, and he was bothering them with all that noise, he stopped and went to bed. Well, now I felt like an ass. Maybe I should go over there tomorrow and apologise for being so brash? It just goes to show, you never truly understand someone else's circumstances from the outside. A little more understanding and compassion would grease the wheel and keep it moving smoother for all of us.

I stared into the darkness of the man's living room for a few more minutes before exhaustion claimed me as well. Too much excitement for one night. I should follow his lead and hit the sack as well. Tomorrow was a brand new day.

* * *

A woman sauntered into my neighbour's living room and did a twirl, taking the place in. "Kinda small, ain't it?" It wasn't the first time I'd seen a woman in his apartment, admittedly, but she was definitely the prettiest.

"Space costs a pretty penny out here. What, you live in a mansion or something?"

"No, no, was just remarking, is all."

He seemed to be in an especially bad mood. Maybe I'd upset him the night before by going over and telling him to keep quiet. I'd gotten up a little earlier than usual to get my study done before his usual antics began.

Sitting before the hole, peeping into another person's existence, a certain calm washed over me that I couldn't explain. He had no idea I could see him, that I knew all his mundane secrets. His daily routine. His mannerisms. The way his eye twitched when he was especially angry. It sent a thrill through me. I was the only one in the world with these secrets. Me, and me alone.

The woman dropped onto his couch and let her bag slip to the floor. She continued looking around, and her eyes fell upon the boxes. "Whatcha got in those?"

He didn't even cast a glance at them as he walked past to the kitchen. "None of your concern."

"Alright, I was just asking, geez."

What *did* he have inside those boxes? It was a good question. They were, for the most part, old and tattered, with some newer boxes on top. The top box stood at around head height, and they were piled carefully so they somewhat resembled a mountain. A mountain of boxes containing something mysterious in the corner of the man's living room. It was the one thing I hadn't been able to figure out yet.

"So, you got 60 minutes, yeah? That started the moment I walked in the door."

The man returned and handed her a glass with clear liquid in it. She held her hand up and shook it. "Drinks aren't part of the deal."

"Take it." His voice was so low it grumbled, almost echoing through the hole.

"We don't drink on the job. I'm sure you can guess why."

On the job? On the... oh. For a moment shame washed over me, peeking in on what would soon be a very private moment, and yet... I still couldn't turn away.

"Are you saying I'm trying to spike your drink? Is that it?"

The woman smiled, but her foot started tapping quickly. She was nervous. My eyes flickered between the two. It was like watching a TV drama, but it was right here in front of me.

"No, of course not. But rules are rules. We're not allowed to—"

He shoved the drink into her hand and towered over her. Slowly, deliberately, his eyes locked on hers the entire time he placed his own cup to his lips and drained the entire thing. Tiny streams of liquid ran down his chin and over his slightly messy beard.

She forced another smile and held the cup up. "Cheers..." She took a small sip. He watched her in silence, unmoving, until she finished the entire thing. Then he took the cup and returned to the kitchen.

The woman looked around the room, her eyes darting here and there, perhaps looking for a way out if it came to that. She checked her phone and quickly put it back in her bag when he returned. She plastered the fake, nervous smile on her face again.

"So, uh, let's get to it, shall we? Was there anything special you wanted, or just a regular?" Her voice trembled as she forced the words out.

"Oh, there's something special I want alright." The way he looked down at her made my skin crawl. Suddenly this seemed bad. Very, very bad. Bad enough to run over and knock on the door, make up an excuse like I needed to borrow some sugar or something. Sure, it was after 1 a.m., but uh, who was to judge when someone needed to bake a cake in the big city, right?

Yet I knew I was being stupid. The man was clearly rough around the edges, but as he'd proven last night, he was also reasonable. He quietened down when asked. Maybe he didn't know how to interact with others very well and this was just his way of doing it. I could empathise with that. I wanted to be a doctor, but dealing with more than a few people at once still set me on edge as well.

"O-Okay, but just so you know, there are limits to—"

She never got to finish the sentence. Faster than lightning he grabbed her around the neck, getting down onto one knee as he pushed her down to the ground, his hands squeezing tighter and tighter, cutting off her flow of air.

The woman flailed, knocking the coffee table over and sending books and mugs flying everywhere. She kicked, landing a solid blow to the man's stomach, but he didn't even flinch. He pushed down harder, slamming her head into the ground a single time as though to say "stop that!"

I couldn't stop the gasp that escaped my lips, but the woman was flailing and kicking so much that neither of them heard me. That was probably for the best. I was witness to an assault in progress. An assault that was no doubt going to turn into a murder.

Murder.

Oh my god.

I couldn't tear my eyes from the hole. The woman. I had to help the woman. I fumbled around blindly for my phone. It had to be somewhere in my pocket. Keeping my eye on her, I grabbed something rectangular and yanked it out of my back pocket. Yes, there it was.

Adrenaline coursed through my veins. The woman gasped and gurgled. Her face turned red. It matched his as he leaned over her, pushing down and squeezing the life out of her. He *was* a murderer. I knew it!

The woman's right arm reached out, looking for something, anything to grab as leverage. She found the boxes. They came tumbling down, and the contents spilt out onto the ground.

I recoiled in horror.

Skulls. Boxes and boxes of skulls. Some animal, some human. The woman's eyes widened even further when she saw them, and the man grinned.

"It's my hobby, you see," he grunted, his biceps bulging as he squeezed. "There's just something about them, and you'd be surprised how big the market is for a freshly cleaned skull. The other bones, they don't go for so much." He stopped for a moment to catch his breath. "But skulls. People love those. Human ones especially."

My hands trembling, I tried to look down at my phone while not tearing my eyes off the sight before me. Skulls. The boxes were full of skulls. An actual mountain of them, now spilt across the floor while he worked on his latest project.

Where were the god damned numbers? Police... Needed to call the police...

"Fuck!" I dropped the phone and tore my eyes away from the hole for just a second. I smashed "110" into the keyboard and pressed my eye back to the hole. The woman's body twitched. Her struggles died down. She didn't have much time left. The police would never get here in time. Even if I ran over and rang the doorbell, who was to say that he would answer? That he wouldn't drag me in and murder me as well.

"Police, what's your emergency?" A female voice filtered out of the phone.

"Yes, hello, there's a woman being murdered!" I covered the phone as I spoke, trying to keep my voice as low as possible.

"I'm sorry, did you say a murder?"

"Yes! Send cars, quickly! Lots of them!"

"Sir, where are you?"

"Higanbana Heights! It's my neighbour! Room 504."

There was a pause on the other end. I turned back to the hole. The woman had stopped moving.

She was dead.

"Understood. Officers will be there shortly."

I dropped the phone and pressed myself as close to the hole as I could. Oh my god. He killed her. He actually killed her. I was looking at the body of a woman who, just moments ago, had been full of life. Now she was empty. Nothing. Gone.

And I did nothing to stop it.

No, I couldn't do anything. What was I supposed to do? Run over and get murdered myself? The boxes were full of skulls! The man was a stone-cold murderer, and this clearly wasn't his first rodeo! There was nothing I could do. Any attempt at help would have resulted in my own death as well. That wouldn't help anyone.

I lived next to a murderer. All those late night noises, were they... were they him killing other people? All this time I thought he was just inconsiderate, and yet...

Someone knocked on the man's door. I almost jumped out of my skin. Holy shit, the police were fast! I'd only called them a minute ago. The man stood up, his gaze flicking between the dead woman on the floor and the door. He dragged her behind the couch so she was hidden and then removed the door chain.

This was it. They'd ask to come in, find the woman's body, and he'd be out of here. My heart pumped so wildly I feared it might burst out of my chest. He was going down. No saving him now!

"What?"

I blinked. I blinked again. I rubbed my eyes and pressed my face so hard against the hole my eyeball almost went right through.

"…What the fuck?" The man turned to look at me, as though he'd heard the sound, and then back to the person standing at the door.

Me. It was… me.

"I, uh, I'm from next door…" My words trailed off as I rubbed my hands together and looked anywhere but at the man.

That was me. Last night. But… how? What? Nothing made sense. The woman lay still behind the couch, trickles of blood running out her nose and mouth. How could I be in two places at once? What was—

"…And?"

The me at the door smiled nervously, lips twitching and hands fidgeting. Oh my god, that was what I looked like to other people?

"…And I noticed you've been, uh, a little noisier than usual lately. I'm trying to study, and—"

The door slammed in my face. Exactly as it had last night. The man walked away and stood in the middle of the room, watching as my shadow passed by the window and disappeared. He sighed, turned to look at the woman, and scratched his head.

"Fucking punk." He knelt down next to the woman, less than a metre from the hole. I recoiled from it. All he had to do was turn around and he would notice it. How he hadn't noticed it all this time astounded me, but if he turned around and saw me looking through it… it would all be over.

But more importantly… what the fuck? I was just at his front door. Yet I was here, in my living room. It played out exactly as it had the night before. No, it didn't play out like the night before. It *was* the night before.

I was watching the past. It hit me like a bolt of lightning. Like an apple on the head, opening my eyes to the truth. Whatever the hole was, it wasn't normal. Maybe... maybe there wasn't even a hole on his side to begin with. Maybe that was why he hadn't noticed. It had appeared suddenly one day, and I'd never thought much more of it. The hole was supernatural in origin. It was letting me see into his world, for what reason I didn't know, and even more strangely, it was showing me the past. 24 hours delayed, like an old security tape.

...The woman was already dead. She died last night, right before I knocked on his door. Those were the sounds I heard.

Oh my god.

Everything came crashing down. The police. They were too late. They wouldn't find anything when they got there because he'd already had 24 hours to clean up his mess. And now... now he knew that I lived here. That I'd heard him. That I knew he was up to something.

I stuck my eye back to the hole and screamed. A bloodshot eye looked back at me, twitching.

"You saw, huh?" His voice was low and deep, so low I almost didn't hear it. Yet it chilled me to my core.

There was a bang at the door. I jumped again, falling back on my ass. A figure appeared at the window, trying to look in. I recognised that hair. It wasn't the police... It was him. He was holding something.

A knife.

I turned back to the hole. The man was dragging the woman's limp body towards the kitchen, his eyes on the hole the whole time. He knew it was there. For the first time, he'd realised the hole was there, and he realised what that meant. I'd seen everything. All along, I'd seen it all.

And now I was next.

The door buckled as he kicked it. I screamed.

The police wouldn't get here in time. By the time they did, he would have broken in and my body would be full of holes. He intended for me to be the next in his skull collection, some rare and exotic trade he carried out in the big city.

But he didn't know the police were coming. My heart pounded like a jackhammer and, as I looked down, I realised I'd wet myself. The police would be too late, but they *were* coming.

I jumped and closed my eyes as the door finally burst open. They wouldn't be too far away now. Maybe even downstairs at that very moment. Not quick enough to save me, no, but as the cold steel silently entered my chest, I took small satisfaction in that my neighbour's skull collecting days would end here. I would be his last victim.

"You stupid or something?" He said, thrusting the knife in again. "I actually didn't think you'd still be here. Guess all that study you did didn't make you as smart as you think."

The blade passed through my ribs. That was the one. I knew it the moment I felt it. The cut that would end my life.

Footsteps on the stairs. Numerous footsteps.

I smiled. Blood trickled down my chin.

"What's so funny?"

I raised a trembling hand, pointing to the door. He turned around and his eyes widened in horror. It was the last sight I would take with me, and as police noticed the open door and the blood-covered man holding a knife inside, they rushed him.

Everything went black.

I'd been too slow to save the woman. Too slow to save myself. But now, thanks to the hole, it was finally all over.

Guess I didn't have to worry about med school anymore.

APARTMENT 807

"Kokkuri-san?"

"Yeah!"

"Are you special?"

"What?"

"Why on earth would you want to play Kokkuri-san?"

Hikari, Kenji, and Izumi sat around my square coffee table in the middle of the living room. A movie buzzed quietly in the background, but nobody was watching it.

"Because it's summer! Come on!" Hikari, for some reason unknown to man, wanted to play Kokkuri-san. I got it, he was an aspiring writer, he liked trying all sorts of things he could include in his work, but Kokkuri-san? Really? Might as well stand on the veranda and scream, "Hey, this guy believes in ghosts, what a moron!"

"What, so the spirits only come out in summer, is that it?" I couldn't hide the scepticism in my voice.

"Huh? No, I never said that. But summer is the season!"

I cast a glance at Kenji and then Izumi, sitting to my left and right. "And you guys?"

Kenji leaned back on his hands and shrugged. "Sure, why not? I don't believe in any of that nonsense, and the quicker he sees nothing's going to happen, the quicker he'll shut up and we can finally move on." See, I knew there was a reason I liked him so much.

"Izumi?"

She, on the other hand, scrunched her face up. "That's kid's stuff."

"You're afraid." Hikari poked her. She grabbed his finger and twisted it back, unrelenting as he squealed in pain. Nobody jumped forward to help.

"Ow ow, let go, let go!"

"And you're stupid. Do you really believe you can summon a spirit to answer your dumb questions?"

"It's just for fun, geez. You don't have to take everything so seriously."

"You should maybe try taking something seriously once in a while. Might be a nice change of pace for you."

The pair glared at each other, and I held my hands between them. "Alright, alright! Kenji's right. He's not gonna shut up until we do it, so let's do it."

It was a hot Friday night. The four of us, friends since childhood who all just happened to end up at various universities in Tokyo, had been having these weekly gatherings since I moved here. They had, to be fair, gotten a little stale.

"What could you possibly want to ask a spirit anyway?" I asked as Hikari smiled and grabbed some paper from his bag. He started drawing up the Kokkuri-san sheet, his messy letters quickly filling the page. He drew a crude shrine gate at the top between "yes" and "no" and plonked it on the table.

"Oh, you know. Stuff."

"Stuff. Uh huh."

"Anyone got a 10 yen coin?"

Kenji fished around in his pocket and flicked a coin towards Hikari. "Keep it. I don't want no cursed coin back."

"I thought you didn't believe in this stuff."

"I don't. But I still don't want no cursed coin."

Hikari smiled. He and Kenji had been best friends since the first grade. Izumi and I had been best friends since the fifth grade. Now we were all thick as thieves, the four of us against the world. Or the big city. Whatever.

"It'll only be cursed if we don't end the game properly. Don't worry, I know what I'm doing."

"Last time you said that, we ended up lost and tailed by some yakuza in the seedy part of town, remember?"

"How was I supposed to know those girls were working?"

"They told you their price right up."

"Yes. Well."

"Boys. Seriously." Izumi glared at them both. They ponied up fake smiles and Hikari placed the 10 yen coin on the paper.

"Anyway. Let's get this game started! Remember, once we start, you can't take your finger off the coin, no matter what happens. Got it?"

"And if I do?" Izumi raised an eyebrow.

"Enjoy being cursed, I guess."

She rolled her eyes. Not even Hikari believed in this sorta stuff, yet here we were.

"Alright, close your eyes. I'll summon the spirit. And remember—"

"Don't take our fingers off the coin, yeah yeah," everyone said in unison.

"Right. Okay, were we go. Kokkuri-san, Kokkuri-san, please come, please come."

I fought the urge to giggle. This was ridiculous.

"Kokkuri-san, Kokkuri-san, if you're here, please move the coin to 'yes'."

I opened a single eye to look at the table. Kenji and Izumi were doing the same. We shared a smile.

"Kokkuri-san, Kokkuri-san!" Hikari continued unawares. "If you're here, please—" The coin started to move. I turned to Kenji and raised an eyebrow. He shrugged. I turned to Izumi. She shook her head. All three of us turned to Hikari. He opened his eyes and beamed.

"Holy shit! It's working!"

"Oh buzz off, that's you moving it yourself."

Hikari furiously shook his head. "I'm not doing a thing! Seriously!"

The coin floated to the hastily drawn "yes."

"Okay, okay. Calm down. This is fine. This is cool. This is exactly what we wanted. Okay. Okay. Questions. A question. Uh…" Hikari started rambling. "Kokkuri-san, will I pass my midterms."

Izumi rolled her eyes. "You invite a spirit and that's what you want to know?"

"Shut up!" Hikari lowered his voice. The coin started moving. Straight across the shrine gate to "no." Hikari's face dropped and Izumi burst out laughing.

"Hey, you asked for that. Maybe this 'spirit' actually does know a thing or two." She thought it was Hikari moving the coin, or perhaps Kenji. It certainly wasn't me, but as I snuck a glance in Kenji's direction, he was smiling. Maybe it really was him after all. It would be just like him to mess with Hikari like that.

"Alright, perhaps that wasn't the best question to ask. Let's try again. Kokkuri-san, let's try something that nobody here will know the answer to. Something only I know. I don't think they believe me yet." He looked straight at Izumi. "Kokkuri-san, what was the name of my pet hamster when I was four-years-old?"

"You had a hamster?" Kenji asked, surprised. Hikari nodded. "I thought you hated animals?"

"I do. Because my hamster died, and I was the one who found him."

Kenji stifled a laugh. The coin was already moving. It stopped a moment on each letter, eventually spelling out "Taro." Izumi burst out laughing.

"You named your hamster Taro? That's... that's beautiful."

"Shut up. I was four. But see! Holy shit. It's true. None of you could have known that."

No-one was impressed. "Uh, Hikari," I said.

"Hmm?"

"Sure, none of us knew that, but you sure did. How do we know that it wasn't you moving the coin to try to convince us that this is real?"

He furrowed his brow for a moment and then his face lit up. "Izumi. You go next. Ask something that only you would know the answer to. If Kokkuri-san gets it right, then that's proof I'm not doing it. Go on."

Izumi sighed. "This is stupid."

"Just do it."

"Fine. Alright, oh great and mighty Kokkuri-san, if you're really here, what did I get for my sixth birthday?"

Izumi had moved to our elementary school in the fourth grade. None of us knew her before then, and we knew little other than she'd moved to the countryside from the city for her father's work.

The coin moved over the letters, one by one, and with each letter it stopped on, Izumi's eyes grew wider and wider.

"Doll bag."

"Holy shit…"

"What?" I sat up straighter, feeling unnerved for the first time.

"I didn't move that, I swear."

"Was it right? Did you get a doll bag?"

Izumi nodded. "I… I treated my doll like a sibling. I was an only child then, Naoki hadn't been born yet…" Her words trailed off for a moment. "I begged my mum for a bag for my doll so I could carry her and her clothes around. I… how?"

Hikari beamed. "I told you. It worked!"

Kenji leaned closer to the table this time. "Alright, my turn. We'll see if this thing is true or not. Kokkuri-san, on the morning of my 16th birthday, my mum made me a special breakfast. What was it?"

He grinned, thinking no-one would be able to guess this one. A doll bag for a little girl's present? Sure, there could be a million things, but it wasn't that huge of a guess. But as the coin started moving, his face dropped.

"Cheeseburger."

"No way..."

I raised an eyebrow. "You had a cheeseburger for breakfast?"

His eyes remained glued to the board. "I... I really like cheeseburgers, okay..." He turned to look at Hikari. "Did you know that? How did you guess?"

Again Hikari smiled. "I told you. It's not me. It's Kokkuri-san."

The room fell silent for a moment. "Go on, Airi, your turn."

I shook my head. "Nah, I'm good."

"Come on, we all went. You need to ask a question as well. It doesn't have to be about your own past. You can ask Kokkuri-san about the future as well, you know."

I sighed and raised both eyebrows. This was stupid. "Fine. Kokkuri-san, will Kenji and I still be together in five years time?"

"Hey!"

I shrugged. "What? It's just a dumb question."

The coin slid over to "no."

"Uh..." Hikari wasn't sure what to say. I raised an eyebrow and looked at the others. "That's not funny. Whoever did that, it's not funny."

All three shook their heads. I turned to Kenji. "Did you do that? Is this your idea of a joke? Because I've put up with a lot from you over the years, but—"

"What? No! Of course I didn't. Why would you even... Hikari!"

He violently shook his head. "Hey, don't look at me! I didn't do it!"

Izumi gulped, her eyes glued to the board.

"Kokkuri-san. Why won't Kenji and I be together in five years time?" I pressed.

"Hey, I don't think you should—" Kenji's words cut off as the coin started moving.

I. Z. U.

I could see where this was going. Something I'd long suspected but never confirmed.

M. I.

I stared at her. She refused to meet my eyes. "Something you wanna tell me?"

She shook her head. Hikari looked confused between the pair and then the light bulb went off.

"Wait, are you two...?"

"This game is stupid!" Kenji went to stand up but Hikari grabbed his hand and kept it glued to the coin.

"What the hell is wrong with you? You can't leave until the game is over!"

"This is all bullshit anyway!" he screamed, but he remained seated. Kenji might not believe in the supernatural, or at least that was what he claimed, but he was still superstitious. His uncle was a monk. Perhaps it stemmed from the weird stories he'd heard over the years.

"Kokkuri-san," I continued. Izumi finally looked at me, her eyes pleading, but I ignored her. "When did my boyfriend fuck my best friend?"

"Airi..."

I ignored the both of them as the coin moved.

"Accident."

I couldn't stop the laugh that escaped my throat. "Are you fucking serious?"

"Airi, please."

"You really fucked her the night she hit her younger brother?"

"It wasn't like that..."

"So what was it like?" Izumi flinched as my voice raised. "What was it like, huh? Izumi got so blind drunk that she decided to take her parents' car for a spin and when her brother tried to stop her, she mistook the brake for the accelerator and ploughed him into the wall, right?"

"Airi, I don't think that's very appro—"

"Shut the fuck up, Hikari." The words were coming out of my mouth, but they weren't my own. Or perhaps there were. Born of years of suspicion and pent up rage that my boyfriend and my best friend were cheating on me behind my back.

"I couldn't stay there that night, remember? My parents and I were flying out the next day. I asked you two to stay with her, to make sure she was okay. She was drunk, after all. Not like she hit and paralysed her brother on purpose." The words spat out like venom, and tears streamed down Izumi's cheeks. "What, did you both fuck her? Is that it?"

"Airi!" This time Kenji raised his voice, but the look on Hikari's face suggested he'd come to understand what was going on as well. Finally.

"I... I went home that night too. I felt uncomfortable after... you know... the thing... and so..."

"And so Kenji and Izumi were home alone. Izumi's poor little brother in the hospital with his parents, unaware he would never get feeling in his legs back because his sister had a little too much to drink, all the while she was back at home fucking her best friend's boyfriend behind her back. Is that how it went? Please, do tell me if I'm wrong."

Neither of them said a word. I couldn't believe it. All these years later and neither of them ever planned to say a thing. They planned to let this continue like nothing was wrong. Like they hadn't betrayed my trust in the worst possible way.

"Kokkuri-san," I continued, raising my voice.

"Airi, please..."

"Are Kenji and Izumi still fucking?"

A sob escaped Izumi's lips. The coin moved to "yes." Again I laughed.

"Of course you are. Of course."

"Airi—"

"What, Kenji? What could you possibly have to say to me right now that I would want to hear?"

He fell silent. Across from him, Izumi whispered something.

"What was that? I didn't hear you." My blood boiled. I wanted nothing more than to toss the two of them over the veranda that very instant. Watch them fall eight floors and laugh as they hit the ground with a satisfying splat.

"I'm sorry..."

"Oh, I'm sure you are. Sorry you got caught. Not sorry you slept with my boyfriend and betrayed my trust for years."

"I was... I was drunk. I didn't even drink that much, I don't know what happened. I... I don't remember much. I was drinking with you guys one moment, next thing I was in the car, then my parents were screaming and then I was in bed with Kenji and..."

Hikari sat stone still, his eyes on the carpet. He'd long had a crush on Izumi. Everyone with eyes knew that. This was no doubt a blow to him as well. She was sleeping with his best friend. The man he trusted his life with. We were both fools.

"Kokkuri-san!" I raised my voice. Everyone turned to look at me, their eyes pleading. Stop. Everyone had had enough. Well, I hadn't. "Kokkuri-san, does Kenji love Izumi?"

"Airi, come on!" Kenji protested, but the coin moved. Slowly, shuddering, before stopping on "no." It didn't make me feel any better. There was a slight vindication and then emptiness once again. Izumi's shoulders slumped.

"Hey, well at least you know now rather than having to wait years to find out like me."

I hated them with every fibre of my being. My entire life had been a lie. They weren't my friends. They were scum that had attached itself to me and I'd been too blind to notice it.

"Nobody else wants a turn? I mean, we're all

here now, getting everything out into the open! Might as well ask!"

Silence.

"Fine. I'll go again. Kokkuri-san. On the night of Naoki's accident, did Izumi really not know what she was doing, as she apparently claims?"

"And what's that supposed to mean?" Finally Izumi spoke. "Are you saying I purposefully hit my brother?"

"I don't know, Izumi! Did you?"

Her eyes screamed bloody murder, but the coin was moving. It stopped on "yes."

"You're out of line," Izumi muttered under her breath. I laughed.

"Rich coming from you."

"Kokkuri-san," Izumi finally interjected. "How many drinks did I have that night? Go on, tell them."

The coin moved and stopped on "2."

"See."

"See what? That just tells me you can't handle your liquor. Two drinks and you got so blind drunk that you don't even remember getting into a car and hitting your own brother before sleeping with my boyfriend. How pathetic."

Izumi furrowed her brow for a moment and then sat up. "Kokkuri-san." Her tone turned inquisitive. "Was there something in my drinks that night that shouldn't have been there? Wait, no, that's confusing. Kokkuri-san, were my drinks spiked?"

The coin moved over to "yes."

Izumi looked around at all three of us. Her drinks were spiked? Who would do that? Why?

"Who spiked my drinks, Kokkuri-san?"

"Hey, guys, we should probably wrap this up soon, yeah, it's getting late and I think we've had enough fun for one night..." Hikari shifted but kept his finger on the coin. A bead of sweat rolled down his cheek.

The coin moved.

H. I. K.

We all turned to look at him.

"Look, this isn't what it looks like..."

"And what does it look like?" This time Izumi screamed. A million thoughts ran through my mind. Hikari spiked Izumi's drinks the night she hit her brother and then slept with my boyfriend? But... why?

"I just... You seemed upset. We were all going to different universities, and you thought it was the last time we'd be able to hang out together like that, and I... I..."

"You what?"

"I just wanted you to relax. To calm down, you know? To have fun..." His voice trailed off.

"Kokkuri-san," this time Kenji spoke. "Did Hikari intend to have his way with Izumi that night?" His voice was low, gruff. His jaw clenched and unclenched the way it always did when he was stressed or angry.

The coin moved to "yes."

Izumi slapped Hikari over the side of his head. "You piece of shit! You drugged me! You drugged me and if Kenji hadn't been there, you would have raped me! Is that it?"

Hikari flinched and shook his head. "No, no! It

wasn't like that at all! I just… I just…"

"You just wanted me passed out so you could have your way with me! You know what that's called, Hikari? It's called rape!"

"I wasn't going to rape you!" Hikari raised his voice for the first time. "I wasn't! I just wanted to lie there with you. But then you got in the car before anyone could stop you, and then… your brother… and when your parents took off to the hospital, I had no idea what was going on and by the time the shock wore off I saw you were already upstairs with Kenji, and…"

"…Wait, you knew?" Hikari looked over at me as I said it. Again he gulped.

"I knew they did it that one time, yes. I… suspected they continued matters, but I wasn't sure…"

"You're just as bad as they are."

"Hey, I didn't—"

"Exactly, that's the problem, Hikari. You never do anything. You sit and wait and let everything happen around you and just hope that something will go your way. I've seen the way you look at Izumi. I've seen the way you look at me. I ignored it, but I damn well saw it, don't worry about that."

His arm trembled and his face twitched. "Kokkuri-san," he said, his voice strained. "Has Airi ever cheated on Kenji?"

Kenji turned to look at me as the coin moved. I kept my eyes straight on Hikari across from me. It landed on "no."

"Fine. Maybe that wasn't the right question. Kokkuri-san, has Airi ever done anything that we don't know about that would break our trust?"

I couldn't stop myself from laughing. "What type of question is that? It's too vague to even get an—" The coin slid over to "yes" without hesitation.

My heart pounded. Three pairs of eyes locked on to me.

"Kokkuri-san," Hikari continued, his voice petulant and angry. "What did Airi do that would break our trust?"

The coin moved. M. U. R.

"Guys, this is stupid, we should—"

D. E. R.

Everyone looked confused. "Murder?" Izumi muttered and turned to look at me. "Wait, what? You killed someone?"

I shook my head. "What? Why on earth would I kill someone? I play the trombone! All my free time is spent with you guys or training for the orchestra! I'm… look at me! How am I even supposed to kill anyone, I'm tiny! What reason would I even have to kill anyone?!"

"That's a good question," Hikari chimed in. "Kokkuri-san, why would Airi kill someone?"

"Whoever is moving the coin better stop it right now, this isn't funny!"

F. U. N.

"Fun? For fun?"

Now *I* was sweating.

"Kokkuri-san, who did Airi kill?" This time Izumi spoke. The coin moved again.

S. T. R.

"Guys…"

"Airi, shut up." I'd never heard that tone of voice coming out of Kenji's mouth before. The surprise made me fall silent.

A. N. G. E. R.

"Stranger? What? You killed a stranger?"

Both my arms trembled. I honestly hadn't expected it to come to this, but here we were. No backing out now.

"It was about six months ago."

"Airi, what the fuck?" Izumi didn't often swear, and again it threw me off balance.

"You *killed* someone?" Kenji said. Hikari remained silent, his previous anger morphing into fear. Yeah, this wasn't the night he imagined when he said he wanted to play Kokkuri-san. Well, you reap what you sow.

"I was walking home from the station. I was on the overpass just after 11 p.m. Someone, I don't know who, attacked me from behind. I think he was a mugger. We struggled. I... I pushed him. He fell over the edge of the bridge, right in front of... in front of a train."

Nobody said a word. "I didn't do it on purpose... It just happened..."

After a few more moments of awkward silence, Kenji finally broke it. "I believe you."

"Look, we really should end this game," Izumi chimed in. "I think we've all said enough for one night, don't you?"

Hikari nodded, sweat pouring down his face. It was hot, but not that hot. "Yeah, good idea. We should probably all go home and get some rest. Everyone's exhausted, that's all. Yeah." Was he trying to convince himself or us?

"Kokkuri-san, Kokkuri-san, please return," he said. The coin moved over to "no."

"Kokkuri-san, please. We don't need you anymore. Please return."

The game couldn't end until the spirit agreed to leave and then we slid the coin across to the shrine gate. But if the spirit refused to leave, then…

"Kokkuri-san, please!" Izumi joined in. "We're done. Please return."

The air around me darkened. A jolt of adrenaline ran through me. The other's voices seemed to fade out for a moment. The room itself faded away, leaving me in a dark bubble, their voices far in the distance.

I understood at once what it was. What it wanted. The spirit didn't want to leave. It had found a kindred spirit. It wanted to stay. It wanted to be free once more. Years of torment, trapped in this building. In this room. I hadn't even known it was there. Or maybe I had. Maybe I liked it. On some subconscious level I knew. And that was why I picked this particular apartment out from all the others.

All I had to do was let it in. Then we'd both be free to do what we wanted. What we *really* wanted.

They betrayed me. They betrayed each other. They weren't my friends. Scum. Parasites that had attached themselves to me that I was too weak to fight off. But it didn't have to be that way. Not anymore. Not since I'd awakened to my true calling. Who I really was. How much I'd *liked* throwing that man over the bridge.

I smiled. One word would end it.

"Yes."

The spirit filled me. Became one with me. Its memories, its history, the bloodlust, the violence, the desire, the pain, it filled me. It matched my own feelings. So long hidden. So long buried. They merged, became one. Finally, we were both free.

They found Kenji, Hikari, and Izumi lying in the parking lot early the next morning. A tragic accident. We'd all been drinking a little too much and when they left the apartment, I went to bed. Little did I know that all three of them had tripped, stumbled, and fallen over the edge of the balcony. Eight floors up. To their doom below.

That was the story we told, anyway. And there was no evidence to otherwise prove that was anything but the truth.

Now that we were one, the real fun was about to begin.

APARTMENT 404

"Tanaka, another order!"

I stuck my head around the corner. Yoneda held up a bag and order receipt.

"And? You're free, aren't you? You deliver it."

"I'd love to, but I'm actually busy. Really busy. You know. There's a big order coming in and I need to wait for it."

I squinted. "I'm sure you can deliver it in the meantime, if the order really is that big."

Typical Yoneda. So lazy.

"It's for Higanbana Heights, okay."

Ah. The light bulb went off. *Now* it all made sense.

"Have fun then!" I returned to the order I was already working on. You didn't see Yoneda picking up the slack in the kitchen to make up for the extraordinary number of orders lately. I was supposed to be a delivery boy. Nothing more, nothing less. Yet the Phoenix Express refused to hire more people, claiming they were "already tight enough as it is." Scummy, more like it.

"Come on, Tanaka. Please. I'll cover your next order. No, your next two orders!"

"If you have that much time then just do it yourself. I'm busy."

"Tanakaaaaaa."

"No."

"Please."

"I said no. I'm working, go away."

"If I disappear, it's your fault, you know." This time Yoneda stuck his head around the corner into the kitchen and pouted.

"That's not very becoming of you, you know."

"Neither is my slow, painful death."

There had been rumours for years that Higanbana Heights was haunted. No delivery drivers wanted to go there. Numerous "incidents" had given it quite the reputation, but I'd never seen or heard anything there, so I didn't know how much truth there was to them. As such, orders for Higanbana Heights usually ended up in my hands, even when it wasn't my order. I was the only one who'd go without a fight.

Well, not today. If they refused to hire more cooks, this was what they got.

"Yeah, yeah, well I'll apologise to your ghost when that happens, okay?"

"You're a meanie."

"Bye, Yoneda."

* * *

Yoneda never returned. 30 minutes after he was scheduled to be back, there was no word from him. The boss called him, but nothing. Just a message that his phone couldn't be reached. At first I thought he was just playing a joke. A little prank to get back at me for not going over there in his stead. But closing time came and still no word. A full day passed. Two days passed. A week passed. No sign of him anywhere. His parents were worried sick and called the store daily to no avail. Something sat lodged firm in the back of my throat, making it difficult to swallow.

My guilt.

If I had just taken the order like he asked me to, none of this would have happened. Yoneda would be standing by the main counter as always, chatting up the staff and waiting for the next order to deliver. He was still young, naïve, and brought a unique energy to the store whenever he burst through the door. Now it was gone, and it was my fault.

If I had just taken that order, Yoneda would still be here.

* * *

"Tanaka. Order."

The cook's voice drew me back to the real world.

"What? Yes, of course. Where to?"

"Higanbana."

My stomach dropped. The cook shrugged and turned back to the kitchen. He had better things to worry about. Still no word on Yoneda. Almost a month had passed. Police had reportedly searched Higanbana Heights and interviewed numerous residents, but nobody had seen him and there was no sign he'd even arrived there.

Somewhere between Phoenix Express and Higanbana Heights, he'd vanished off the face of the planet. Only, people didn't just vanish. They went somewhere, either of their own volition or against their free will. Yoneda had no reason to run away, so that meant...

"You gonna deliver that or what?"

The staff member manning the register looked at me. I smiled and nodded. "Yeah, no. Of course. Sorry." I held the bag up, showing that I was on my way, and the door tinkled as I exited. A large order of noodles with extra meat and a side order of dumplings. My stomach grumbled. The one bad thing about working as a delivery boy was the smell, especially if you were hungry. Sometimes it took all I had not to tear into the food right then and there.

I jumped on my bike and hit the road. They hadn't even found Yoneda's bike, and the bosses seemed to be more upset about that than the young man riding it. Those bikes aren't cheap to replace, you know, they said. And they had to get all new signage and registration done, also not cheap, they said. Money money money. A man had gone missing and all they gave a shit about was their bike.

Maybe it was time to find a new job. Plenty of other delivery joints around the place. At least one of them had to give a shit. At the very least, they had to pay better than Phoenix Express. Bottom of the barrel scum suckers.

I should pay Yoneda's parents a visit on my way back, I thought. We'd never been the closest of friends, but they deserved every bit of support they could get. They certainly wouldn't get any from work. Plus... I swallowed. It should have been me. I should have gone.

I pulled up in front of Higanbana Heights. A large, dirty building rose high into the sky before me. It was certainly creepy. Hard to deny that. Dark stains that looked like blood seemed to drip down from one of the windows on the upper levels. They really couldn't get someone to clean that up? Blood, mould, whatever, it was gross, and it was creepy.

There were only two cars in the parking lot. I always wondered how the building managed to stay in business. I almost never saw more than a handful of cars there, yet there were eight rooms to a floor, so, what, 64 apartments in all? The place was a dump. Hard to blame them.

I checked the order receipt. Room 404. The sun sat low in the horizon on the other side of the building, casting me in its shadow. Best hurry it up and get on my way before it got dark.

I pressed the button for the elevator, but it was on the top floor. I waited and waited, but it showed no signs of moving. Ugh. Whatever, the order was on the fourth floor. It wasn't that far in the grand scheme of things, and they'd dock me if I took too long. Plus the customers would complain if the food was cold. The stairs were right there. Think of it as free exercise, I told myself.

As I climbed, I wondered if Yoneda had reached this far. Had he climbed these very same stairs before disappearing? Where did he go after that? Did a tenant kidnap him? They said this place was full of the worst of the worst. Only drug dealers, murderers, yakuza, etc etc lived in Higanbana Heights. I'd delivered meals to students, young single women, the elderly, I knew that wasn't true... but still.

Where had Yoneda gone?

Speak of the devil, a group of four students passed me as I reached the third floor. They were involved in an intense argument over the best type of beer to pick up from the convenience store. 'Ah, to be young again,' I thought, having only graduated a year earlier myself. And still the only job I could find was delivering shitty take out. Maybe I should have majored in something that would have gotten me a better job, like IT or medicine...

I reached the fourth floor and stopped for a minute. 404. That was the apartment directly to my right. I checked the number on the door and pressed the buzzer. Which apartment had Yoneda visited? Did he make it all the way to the door? They didn't find his bike here, so maybe he hadn't made it this far to begin with.

Maybe he fell off a bridge and both he and his bike were sitting at the bottom of a river somewhere. No, they would have found some evidence of that. Someone would have seen it. At the very least, the food would have eventually floated to the surface and people would have found the bag. Right?

I pressed the buzzer again. No answer. I double checked the receipt and the numbers on the door. Definitely 404. I snickered. Not found. Haha. I'd probably do the same thing if I lived in 404. Pretend I wasn't home just to fuck with drivers who no doubt doubted themselves when seeing the address.

A chill settled over the area and I shivered. The sun wasn't fully gone, but in the shade of the building it might as well have been. Not like I could see it, anyway.

"Hello? Phoenix Express." I knocked on the door three times, hard. "I have your delivery." I pressed my face to the window, but I couldn't see anything inside. Just dark curtains and no sign of life or light. I knocked a few more times. "Hello? I have your food!"

My stomach grumbled again. It was tempting to sit down on the veranda right there and start eating it. If they didn't want it, no point letting it go to waste. I'd personally never had a delivery that didn't answer the door, but I'd heard stories from other drivers where, for some unknown reason, they arrived at a place and nobody answered. We were supposed to bring the food back in such cases, but then it would just get thrown out because they couldn't sell it again. If they didn't want it, well, why let good food go to waste, right? They wouldn't know that nobody picked up. The food was already paid for, so the store wasn't losing anything.

I shook my head. No. If they found out I did that they'd dock my wages, and another month of cold showers was not high on my wish list. Plus there was a chance that whoever was inside was caught up and just couldn't reach the door. Maybe they were stuck on the toilet or something. I could leave the food hanging on the handle... We weren't supposed to because anyone could walk by and take it, but I was running out of options.

Pulling my phone out of my pocket, I dialled the store. The phone beeped numerous times. "Huh?" I removed it from my ear. No reception. I looked around. The place suddenly seemed darker. A lot darker. Not like a cloud passing overhead or the sun sinking below the horizon, but the type of darkness where you're lying down and someone suddenly drops a blanket over your head. Everything goes pitch black in an instant. That type of darkness.

"What the hell?" I couldn't even see any stars. No lights from the city. No cars on the road. Everything was... black.

I banged again. "I'm leaving your food here, okay!" I hung it from the door handle and ran over to the elevator. Still at the top floor. I pressed over and over, harder and faster each time. "Come on, come on." The elevator showed no signs of moving.

"What the fuck, man? Come on!"

It was hard to describe the feelings that ran through me as I stared out into pitch darkness, waiting for an elevator that didn't want to move. It was like sitting in a room full of people and suddenly realising that everyone had six fingers except you. Like sitting in a restaurant and realising that everyone was eating raw steak while you were eating salad. Like opening a present from your parents on Christmas Day only to find the box was empty and they were smiling down at you like it was what you'd wanted and asked for all those years. It was… weird. Wrong.

"Screw this." I ran over to the stairs. My stomach grumbled again, loudly this time, but it was oddly comforting. A reminder that some things never changed as my feet pounded down the stairs. They echoed so loud I almost stopped to turn back a few times to see if someone was following me, but I couldn't. I just wanted out of there as quickly as possible.

Yet, no matter how much I descended, I never reached the bottom. When I hit the next floor, I went to check where I was and stopped dead in my tracks. The Phoenix Express bag hung from the door handle. I was still on the fourth floor.

"What the actual fuck?"

I ran back to the stairs, this time going up. Every time I hit a floor that Phoenix Express bag hung from the door handle, mocking me. I dropped to my knees, tears threatening to spill forth. What on earth was going on?

The sky seemed even blacker than before. A pure void that wasn't actually black, but more an absence of any light. There should be stars out there. A moon. City lights. Something. Yet there was only a void. I looked at my watch. It was frozen on 7:24 p.m. Not even the second hand ticked. Still too early for this type of darkness, even if we removed the stars from the equation.

"Okay, okay, calm down." The words seemed to echo all around me. I banged on the door again.

"Hello? Is anyone there?" Still nothing. "If you don't answer, I'm going to force my way in. Please, if you're there, answer me!"

Silence. Silence coming from the apartment, anyway. My ears prickled. Something behind me was... shuffling? Dragging something? I froze and all the hairs on my arms stood on end. I had to turn around. I couldn't but I had to. Something at the end of the floor was shuffling closer. It could be a tenant. They might know what the hell was going on.

But it also might not be. Deep down in my bones I knew it. This was what happened to Yoneda. He had a delivery for the fourth floor. He had to have. I had no proof of that, but what else explained it? He came here and then disappeared. Maybe he was still stuck here somewhere too? Maybe that was Yoneda behind me?

I turned around. For better or worse, I had to know. "Yoneda!" I screamed before I could stop myself.

It wasn't Yoneda. It wasn't even human at all.

A panicked scream escaped my throat and I banged on the door a few more times. "Hello! Open up! Open up, dammit!"

Something vaguely human in shape shuffled towards me, dragging what looked like a broken ankle behind it. It could have been human once. It was hard to tell. At the very least, it was human shaped. A head. Two arms. Two legs. Dark, ashy skin. A little too grey to be human, but I didn't know, maybe there were sicknesses that could do that, I was no doctor.

But... it was entirely featureless. Nothing that even resembled a nose, eyes, a mouth. Just a flat, featureless space where a face should have been.

And then it moaned.

How it moaned without a visible mouth was beyond me, but I wasn't sticking around to figure it out. I removed the food from the handle and took a step back before kicking the door. It rattled loudly, as I thought it would. This place was old and falling apart. I gave it another kick, and this time it cracked, although it remained shut. One more should do it. What I planned to do once I was in there, who knew, but I couldn't hang around out here any longer.

Crack. The door burst open with a deafening bang and I followed it in, slamming it behind me. There was a TV stand by the wall. I ran over to it, pushing it towards the door to block the entrance I'd just made. The TV fell with an unceremonious crash and again the echo hurt my ears. Why was everything so loud all of a sudden?

I dropped the bag of food and ran to the hall, hiding behind the corner. I had probably two minutes to think myself out of this situation. The shuffling grew louder, but with how off everything sounded here, it would be difficult to judge just how far away that thing was.

Could it even see me? Did it even know I was here? My heart pounded wildly. Maybe it didn't even know I was there, and when I kicked the door in, I alerted it to my presence. Idiot!

Okay, time for berating myself later. First things first. What now? I ran over to the kitchen door. It opened to a small balcony that overlooked another mostly empty car park four stories below. Void surrounded the area. Well, I couldn't jump down. That would be instant death.

The shuffling grew louder. Maybe that would be preferable to whatever that thing was. I looked up but only saw more balconies above. Climbing higher probably wouldn't do me much good if I was even that athletic in the first place. I wasn't. Maybe I could climb down and drop onto the next balcony?

No. I'd likely miss and fall to my painful death below. An option if it came down to that or the monstrous being out the front, but not quite yet.

Another moan. Again the hairs on my arms stood on end. It was guttural and primal, awakening something inside me that I could only describe as pure terror.

Think. Come on. Think.

The lights in front of the apartment flickered. Each time they did, it plunged me into total darkness. I never realised what total darkness really meant. No matter where you went, there was always some type of light. A distant street light. A star in the sky. The electronic display on an appliance. Ambient light from something. Yet when those lights went out, they took everything else with them. Pure darkness. No escape.

My phone. I grabbed it again, dropping it to the floor with slippery fingers. "God dammit. Come on." I pressed the home button with a shaky hand and the screen lit up. "Oh, thank god." I dialled work again, the first number on the list. Nothing happened. Of course it didn't, not only was there no reception, there was nothing at all. The top of the phone was empty. No bars, no carrier, nothing.

"Fuck!" I threw it across the room. As the lights flickered again, my stomach dropped. I hadn't been paying close attention, so I hadn't noticed, but each time they went out, the apartment changed. It was subtle. Subtle enough to miss it, but now that I had noticed it, it was unmistakable.

The walls grew dark. The ceiling warped and bowed. The floor rotted beneath my feet. Tiny pieces of wood crumpled off the empty kitchen table.

The apartment was decaying.

I grabbed the bag of food I'd dropped and emptied it on the floor.

"Oh, oh god..." Maggots crawled throughout the food and the noodles had turned a horrific shade of green and black. Everything around me was decaying. I checked my arms in a panic and frantically touched my face. Was I decaying too? What did that even mean for a live human? Would I rot like the food and walls? Would I just get old and wrinkly? Would I wither into a pile of bones and dust?

I jumped. There it was again, that moan. The shuffling stopped outside the door. Maybe if I remained quiet, it wouldn't notice me. It didn't have eyes. Ears. A mouth. Its leg was broken. How would it even get in?

I crawled down the hall, keeping low and making as little noise as possible. I tested all the doors. The bathroom was locked, yet the two rooms opened. Dead ahead was the bedroom while the door to my right looked like an office.

Okay. My options were thinning, but there were still options. One, I could jump out the bedroom window to my death. Not ideal. Two, I could hide in the bedroom closet. Not an immediate death, but if the thing out there came inside, well, there weren't many places to check. I'd be trapped in a tiny space and face to face with a monster. Also not ideal. Third, I could jump out the home office window, taking me back to the front balcony and then... what? I'd still be alive, sure, but that just removed me from the apartment and put me in a larger open space in the same situation.

Dammit.

Part of my decision was removed for me. The door in the living room burst open. I covered my ears and slammed the home office door behind me. Out the window it was. Stay alive, sort the rest out later. The room looked as though it had been abandoned for decades. I picked the chair up to toss at the window and it crumpled upon impact.

"Oh, that's just wonderful."

I reached for the lock, but it was rusted tight. Nothing in the room was sturdy enough to break through it. I removed my delivery jacket and wrapped it around my wrist. Here goes nothing.

I wasn't quite sure what to expect, but the massive pain running down my forearm upon impact wasn't really it. The glass cracked but didn't shatter. A heavy duty window, no doubt because it faced the public balcony.

The shuffling got closer. It was right by the door. If it didn't know I was in here before, it certainly did now.

"Come on!" I braced myself and hit the window again. The cracks grew larger and more jagged. Fantastic. If I managed to break through, there was also a good chance I'd slash my entire arm doing it.

The door banged behind me. I jumped and shrieked. Another bang. Pieces of dead wood fell to the floor. Another bang. They sounded like gunshots right by my ear. Another and the creature was through.

Up close it was horrific. I had been right in that there were no features, but now that it was right in front of me, I could see that wasn't entirely correct. It had a face. Trapped somewhere beneath the pale, pulsating skin that made up its head. Eyeballs shifted where there were no eyeballs. A mouth tried to open where there was no mouth. I stared at it in horror and disgust, for a moment forgetting myself. Even its broken ankle, twisted in an all too wrong direction, had been healed over with the dark ashy skin.

And then it hit me.

"Oh my god…"

An off-colour on its chest drew my attention. It moaned again and I withdrew further into the window, hoping to fall through it. Disappear into the ether. Get the hell away from there as quickly as possible.

Two characters. Characters I knew very well. I shared one of them in my own name.

Yoneda. It was Yoneda's name tag from his delivery jacket. Fused or merged into his skin or something. It was swallowing him whole. The moans weren't coming from its mouth. It had no mouth. They were coming from *Yoneda* beneath it.

"Yoneda..." My voice cracked. "What... what is..."

The lights flickered. The room degraded. They flickered again. The wall felt both sticky and crumbly to the touch. Yoneda, the thing, whatever it was, dragged his broken ankle closer, closing in on me.

Another flicker. The colours on the name tag faded. The creature reached out for me. The lights went out, plunging us into darkness. I screamed. At least, I think it was me. Something gooey grabbed my neck.

"Ta... na... ka..." That was what it sounded like. Perhaps it was nothing but a moan. Perhaps I was hearing what I wanted to hear. The name tag was gone. Nothing but a dark, ashy, featureless shape stood before me, its arms wrapped around my neck. A cold sensation spread throughout my body. The lights flickered again. Only this time when they came back on, they were still shrouded in darkness. Cloudy. Musty.

Yoneda didn't disappear. He was trapped. The building had claimed him. Turned him into whatever monstrosity stood before me.

"Yoneda... I'm sorry..."

And now he was no longer alone.

Would they look for me too when I never returned? Or would they simply complain about losing yet another bike and sent a different delivery man out here? One after the other, wondering why they never came back. To a floor on a cursed

building that didn't exist.
    Not in *their* world, anyway…

APARTMENT 602

"You shouldn't be keeping your trash in there, you know."

I cringed. The voice immediately gave away who was standing behind me. The nosy bitch from the second floor. Preparing myself, I turned around and forced a smile.

"Mrs Ito." She hated when I called her that. She wasn't married, and she knew that I knew. The dance had begun. "You look lovely this morning." She didn't.

"Don't give me that. You know you're not supposed to keep trash down here. It attracts all sorts of pests." Like her, apparently.

"It's trash day the day after tomorrow. There's nowhere to keep it in my apartment and—"

"And what? The rules don't apply to you? We all make do! Everyone does what they can to abide by the rules, if we don't, then what do we even have?"

Less trash in my apartment?

"I'm terribly sorry." I forced the smile again, fully aware I no doubt looked to be having an aneurysm. "It won't happen again."

She gave me the once over and then turned her eyes to the door. "What do you have in there, anyway? You should keep that place clean, you know. All we need is one rat and then the whole place is swarming with them."

Wasn't that the truth?

"Just some furniture and things I can't fit upstairs." What the hell did it matter to her what I kept in my storehouse anyway? I could have a meth lab in there, for all it mattered to her. Nosy bitch. She lived by the stairs on the second floor and seemed to spend most of her time patrolling or watching those coming and going like she was some sort of caretaker. Stupid old woman. There was no caretaker. Like anyone would be stupid enough to work here.

"Well, you make sure to keep it clean. If I find any rats—"

"I know, you'll call the landlord." Same conversation every time. Didn't she have better people to hassle than me? I waited until she shuffled off and tossed the trash bags in the storehouse. I wasn't dragging that stuff all the way back upstairs. Screw what she thought. Only two more days until trash collection, and the bags were tied. Ugh, she boiled my blood.

She was right about one thing though. The storehouse could use a clean. They weren't very large, but they were big enough for each resident to store an old deck table and chairs, a few boxes etc that wouldn't fit in the actual apartments. And yes, we weren't supposed to keep trash in them either, but the alternative was leaving it on my balcony to rot in the summer heat. That wouldn't be ideal for anyone.

"Oh yeah, the can opener." Leaving the door open a crack, I rustled through some boxes looking for my long-lost can opener. I'd managed to buy the one can in the entire supermarket that didn't come with a pull-tab. Who even did that anymore? How was that convenient?

An unknown box at the bottom of the pile caught my eye. "Hmm? And what might you be?" I marked all my boxes with what was inside, yet this one was blank. I pulled it out and opened the top.

"...Tapes?" Who even had a video player anymore? "These aren't mine..." I looked around, half expecting someone to jump out and claim the mystery box, but no-one did. Not even Ms Ito. I was the only one with the key to this storeroom, so how...?

"Well, finder's keepers! Might as well check out what's on them!" I stuck my head around the corner to see if anyone was watching. Confirming the coast was clear, I closed the door behind me and ran for the elevator. My heart pounded like a jackhammer and I had to stop myself from jumping up and down on the ground in giddiness. Finally, some excitement. What could be on the tapes? Old home videos? Long lost TV shows? Someone's school project? I didn't even care. Something new and exciting to break up the drudgery that was my life. Just what the doctor ordered.

There was, of course, one problem. I plopped the box of tapes in the corner of the room and turned towards the TV. I didn't have a video player. I did, long ago, but I got rid of it when I upgraded to my DVD player. Maybe the secondhand store would have one? They had everything. I could buy technology made long before even my parents were born in those things.

Alright. On my way home from work the following day, I'd stop by and pick one up. Maybe it would help pass yet another boring day in the office faster, knowing that something exciting waited at the end of it. What could be on the tapes? It took all I had not to run out the door that very instant and buy a tape player immediately. The store would no doubt be closed by the time I got there. I'd just have to suck it up and wait.

Oh, the excitement!

* * *

I plonked my brand spanking new (several decades old) video tape player on the table. It consumed my mind the entire day and by the time 5 p.m. rolled around, I didn't even realise it was the end of the workday. I sped out the door before my boss could ask me to do some inevitable overtime and made my way straight to the closest secondhand store I could find.

There it sat, like holy light beaming down on it. A dusty, crappy old video player. Probably hadn't seen usage for at least a decade, but it was cheap and, according to the staff member at the cashier, still working. That was all I needed.

I plugged it in and reached out for the first tape with a shaky hand. This was it. The big moment. Finally, I would discover what secrets lay in these mystery tapes. Where they came from, nobody knew. What they hid, I was about to find out.

It was like being in a mystery novel!

I put the first tape in and pressed play. Here we go!

The screen went dark and fuzzy lines crossed it. Ah, the old 80s and 90s aesthetic. Nice. A man walked through a forest in first person view. The camera turned as he turned his head, looking side to side as though searching for something. I didn't recognise the area. I scooted closer to the TV, immediately drawn in.

Suddenly the man stopped and turned around. Was that a noise? Yes. A breaking tree branch. The man started running. His arms appeared in and out of frame as he ran. How did they do that? It had to be one of those cameras they mount on your forehead. There were no credits or any sort of text at the start of the video though, so it didn't seem to be a professional movie. Maybe homemade? Students?

The man turned into the trees. He held an arm up, protecting against the branches that grasped for his face. One slashed his arm, causing a tiny stream of blood to trickle down it.

"There!" I shouted before I could stop myself. Up ahead, a figure ran through the trees. He was after whoever that was. Why?

The camera shook, and the figure turned around

before running straight into a tree and hitting the ground. That was all the man needed. He quickly closed the distance and his hands fell upon the person's neck. It was a young man, and his eyes bulged and face turned red as the man squeezed harder and harder.

"How did they do that?" I wondered. A trickle of blood poured from his nose and he gasped, the veins in his neck popping out as he turned redder and redder. His arms and legs flailed and kicked, yet the man squeezed harder, grunting with the effort. Finally, after what seemed like an extraordinarily long time, the man fell limp. The killer stood up, turned around, and returned to the main path. He continued on his way as though nothing had happened, and the tape ended.

"Uh..." What the hell was that? Cheap production quality, not much of a story, and the death scene dragged on for far too long. Maybe it was a raw cut for a larger movie. Something they would edit in post-production later. Still... how exciting. How old were these tapes? It was impossible to tell anything from what the man was wearing, and there was nothing else to date it. I might have been the first person in years, no, even decades to watch these.

A chill of excitement ran through me.

"Alright, the next one!" I grabbed the next tape in the box and put it in, dancing side to side in my seat. What would this one hold?

The same black screen and fuzzy lines crossed the screen, and then the darkness slid up. It was the same first person point of view as the previous tape, but the man wasn't in a forest this time. He stalked some dark alleys, numerous people crossing to and fro as he made his way deeper in.

I squinted, scanning the sign names. Tokyo? It had to be, but I didn't recognise anything yet.

The man walked into a store and the staff bowed as he passed by. He passed through a maze of tight halls, bright red light filling the screen. When he reached the end, three nondescript doors waited before him. The man hesitated a moment before going through the middle one.

He entered a dark room. There was a bed in the corner and an assortment of items on a nearby table. Toys?

Oh? Oh… Recognition washed over me. Adult toys…

"Uh…"

The man sauntered over, running his hands along them before stopping at the end and turning towards the dark corner. It was hard to make out, but suddenly something moved.

A woman. Cowering in the corner. She suddenly screamed.

"Stay away! D-Don't come any closer!"

Yet he did. The woman produced a knife, her hands trembling. The man's step didn't falter even once, and as she thrust it towards him, he snatched it out of her fingers and turned it back on her, thrusting it into her rib cage once, then twice.

"Not really my kinda thing, but at least it looks realistic, I guess," I said as blood trickled down the man's hand. Several boyfriends over the years had made me watch movies like this with them. Not really my taste, but whatever floated their boat.

The man lifted the knife again and this time brought it down on her neck, causing a spurt of blood to fly into the air and coat the camera. Well, the effects were certainly good. He then dropped the knife and placed his hands around her neck, as though trying to wring her blood dry. As the girl lay dying on the ground, choking and drowning in her own blood, it suddenly hit me. The man never spoke. Not once. He grunted, but he never spoke.

Maybe some type of experimental art torture film? Again, not really my thing, but I'd also seen worse.

Then it hit me again. If this was some long-lost art film, or at the very least the raw takes… maybe the tapes were worth money? If I could figure out who they belonged to, and let them know that "hey, I've got your stuff," maybe I could get something out of it?

The tapes were old. By the looks of them, real old. Old enough that even if I couldn't find the real owner, I could probably sell them for a high price to a collector. The cogs in my brain turned as I grabbed the next tape. Maybe this one would give me a hint as to who was behind them.

The scene opened on a site I recognised. It was my workplace. "What the hell?" The man lingered on it before moving on, passing down a familiar alley. The same alley I always took on my way to work. Numerous people passed him… including myself.

I stopped the tape. A shot of adrenaline made me tunnel vision on the TV. No way. I was in the tape.

I looked at the man as he passed by. I looked right at him. Judging by my appearance, it was recent. I certainly didn't remember seeing any camera crew, nor a man with a camera attached to his head.

What was going on?

I took a deep breath, rewound a few seconds, and pressed play.

It was definitely me. No doubt about it. Hard to tell when—I had to wear the same hairstyle to work every day—but it didn't look old. The last few weeks or months, maybe. Again, I looked right at the man as he walked past. He didn't pay any special attention to me, I was just another in the crowd, but I was there. I looked at him.

Who was he?

The scene continued as he went further into the city, through darker and dirtier back alleys. Then he stopped, apparently having found his target. A young woman turned around and her eyes went wide. I tilted my head. She looked vaguely familiar. Did I know her from somewhere? And did she know him?

"Stay away!" she screamed. "This has nothing to do with me! Why me?" She ran, and he chased after her. I didn't recognise where they were. I'd never been into that section of town before. There were few people around, and the few they did pass kept their heads down as the woman screamed for help.

Finally, she was trapped. Stuck between a dead end and the man closing in on her. She threw her bag at him, and the man dodged it.

"What do you want from me?" she screamed, her voice hoarse and laboured. "I know who you are, you know!"

I perked up. She knew? Who was he? The lines between fact and fiction blurred. I had no idea what was what anymore. Were these real tapes? Actual snuff videos? I'd heard of them before, but I always thought they were nothing more than urban legends.

But where was the camera? That part I couldn't explain. Maybe he had a hat on, and there was a hidden camera inside it? It was the only thing that made sense. After all, the tape showed me looking right at him. I'd remember a man with a camera on his head, and I had no memory of any such thing.

And who was this woman? I had definitely seen her somewhere before. But where?

I leaned closer, my heart pounding, waiting to see what happened next.

"I know you left the tapes in my apartment. I know it was you!"

My ears twitched.

"I won't tell anyone! I swear! I'm moving out of that cursed place soon anyway! I'll burn them! I'll pass them on! I'll do whatever you want, but please—" Her cries were cut short. The man crossed the short distance between them, reaching out for her neck and slamming her head into the wall. She gurgled, her eyes opening wide and her mouth opening and closing as she tried to get more words out.

"Please... I won't..." That was the last thing she said. The man slammed her head into the wall again, and then again, and her body fell limp. A dark stain coated the wall as her body slid to the ground with a dull thud. The man leaned down over her, brushing a lock of hair from her face. He turned to look in the puddle beside her. For the first time, I caught sight of the man's reflection and gasped.

He looked... normal. Like an everyday businessman you might see anywhere. He wasn't massively large or buff. If anything he looked a little underweight. He had normal, short cut hair, and no visible scars, marks, or tattoos anywhere. And his face. His face was... perfectly plain. Nondescript. Someone you wouldn't even look twice at in the street.

And then it hit me. A perfectly plain, nondescript face. With no camera attached.

No camera.

I was seeing exactly what he saw.

The man smiled, and the screen went black.

...What the hell?

I took the tape out and left the TV blank for a moment. It was too much to process at once. I had assumed the man was wearing a camera. That this was some sort of art project, the rough cuts of an independent film, I didn't know. Something like that.

But the deaths had been real. A sickening feeling washed over me as I realised. The man in the forest, the woman in the room, the woman in the alley... they were all real people, and he had really killed them. They were snuff films. But he wasn't wearing a camera.

How was he doing it?

And why did I have the tapes? The previous woman had said something about them. *"I know you left the tapes in my apartment."* The man? Why would he leave them? What would that accomplish? Did he leave them in my apartment as well? And why did I feel like I knew that woman?

"Ah, I don't get it!" I slammed the coffee table and jumped as the box jumped with it. A single tape fell out and onto the table.

Dare I do it? One last tape? Maybe the answers were in there. After all, the previous tape had finally shown who the man was, and given me a location I knew.

The room felt unseasonably cold for summer. I looked around, half expecting the man to be standing in the corner, smiling and waiting for me to uncover his dirty secrets. But I was alone, nothing but me, a blank TV, and a video player hungry for a new tape.

I clenched my jaw, readied myself, and put it in.

An all too familiar scene opened up before me. I recognised the location immediately. The main road only a few hundred metres from Higanbana Heights. A few cars passed by, but the roads were mostly empty.

The man turned a corner. He walked at a casual pace, neither running nor dawdling. He rounded another corner, and then another, and with each one my heart beat faster and faster. No doubt about it. He was heading towards Higanbana Heights.

He was coming here.

I looked around the room again, still expecting to see him suddenly standing there, but I was alone. The sun sank behind the buildings as the man walked, slowly getting darker.

The sun outside was setting, casting a soft haze

over my apartment, the final light before day disappeared and night took over.

No way.

He turned another corner, nodding as he passed a woman on the street. At the end of that road he only had to turn one more time and then he would be here. He would be at Higanbana Heights.

I ran to the door to make sure it was locked. I didn't know why, but something compelled me. The man continued his casual pace down the road and I checked the window too. Just in case. I turned back to the TV, and he turned the final corner and looked up.

My blood ran cold. There it was, Higanbana Heights in all its glory. He walked over and stood in front of the building, taking it in. I could almost feel him smile.

Looking closely, I could see my door. My heart pounded in my ears. A door down the end of the hall slammed and I jumped. It was soon followed by footsteps, and then a figure passed the window. I gulped and turned to the TV.

Oh no. No, no, no…

A figure walked passed my window, another resident from down the hall. I watched them, through his eyes, as they passed my apartment and pressed the button for the elevator. He turned to watch them too, and then made his move.

He was down there. It didn't make sense, but it didn't matter. The tape was real time, showing me what he was doing at that exact moment. He was coming up here. He knew where I lived. He knew who I was. I was his next victim.

The resident stepped out of the elevator and he stepped in. I caught his reflection in the elevator mirror before he turned around and pressed a button. The number 6 lit up.

I couldn't tear myself from the screen. My heart pounded and my insides screamed. The door was locked. The windows were locked. It was too late to run now. Cheerful elevator music played and before long it arrived on my floor. The man stepped out. I heard the elevator ping outside my apartment.

He was coming. I looked around the room for a weapon. Anything I could defend myself with. I grabbed my coffee mug, and not a second later the doorbell rang. I squealed and jumped.

Maybe I could hide. Pretend I wasn't home. I froze, doing my best to calm my breathing, to blend into the furniture, to disappear into nothingness. The doorbell rang again. A jolt ran through me. I gripped the coffee mug even tighter.

Go away... There's nobody here... Leave me alone...

This time he knocked. The knocking got louder, angrier, more frequent. The door buckled and creaked. I screamed and ran right as it burst open, dropping the mug behind me. I ran for my bedroom and slammed the door.

"Come on, come on!" I fumbled with the lock, but it was too late. The man stood right before me. No doubt at that very moment, my face was on the TV in the lounge. My eyes wide with fear. My mouth trying to form words my brain couldn't string together.

The man was perfectly nondescript. He reached

out, his hands tightening around my neck. I'd seen him do this to so many people, and now I was on the other end of it. He was strong. Too strong for a regular human.

That woman. It suddenly hit me where I'd seen her before. It was an odd time to think of it, but maybe that was what death was. An incoming rush of thoughts and feelings that made no sense, your brain squeezing out the last little bits it could before it stopped firing entirely.

I'd seen her right here. In this very building, maybe a year or so earlier. She was another tenant. Or, had been another tenant.

Perhaps the other victims had been too. The tapes. The man left the tapes for people to find, each tape detailing a death. A death recorded in real time. Not filmed. Recorded. I couldn't explain it, but finally I understood it.

My tape was recording right now. His hands squeezed tighter and tighter. Soon my neck would snap. My lungs would burst. Blood would trickle from my nose, my mouth, maybe my ears. Something inside my eye exploded.

It was all recording right now, playing back on my TV as it did. Then when he was done, he would leave the tapes for another tenant to find. Maybe not now. Perhaps in a few months. A few years. Someone else would find some mystery tapes and, curious, put them in to watch.

They would see that man's death. The woman's death. Then finally my death. But that wouldn't be the end of it. Then they'd put one more tape in and recognise the man getting closer and closer. If they were lucky and recognised what was happening quickly, they might run. They might end up in a forest. In an alley. Or they might end up trapped in a room, or perhaps staring stupidly at their own TV because they were too slow to notice.

My vision faded. Life left me. A barrage of thoughts, images, and sounds bombarded me, almost like static on a TV as my brain eked out its final sparks.

He would strike again. Once you started watching the tapes, it was too late.

He couldn't be stopped.

APARTMENT 308

MY WHOLE LIFE I'VE SUFFERED from sleep paralysis. "Suffered" really is the best way to put it, because it has often ruined my life. I first experienced it when I was eight-years-old, and I was far too young at the time to understand what it was. I truly thought a demon was trying to drag me down to hell, or that our house was haunted.

My parents weren't much help. They'd tell me it was just a dream and to ignore it and it would go away. It didn't. The paralysis got worse, to the point where I stopped trying to sleep. At eight-years-old I was sneaking cans of soda from the fridge and even had my first taste of coffee. It was gross. I stuck to the soda.

This, of course, took its toll on me and every other day one of my parents got called in from work to deal with the fruits of my labour at school. Those labours generally being disrupting the class, falling asleep in class, and acting out at other kids because

I had no idea what was going on anymore.

Several therapists and a few moves later, the sleep paralysis finally stopped. Not for good, but for a good while at the very least. Then it came roaring back when I was a teenager. I started researching it myself and I realised that not only was I not alone, it was actually quite common, and it affected people in slightly different ways.

Some claimed to see an old hag approaching them, to others it was shadow men. Others saw nothing at all, only a pervasive sense of terror that something was coming for them, and once it got there, it would all be over. Others saw strangers breaking into their home, or long dead family members. The list went on.

Me? I saw shadow men. I hated them. I didn't get any of that "sitting on my chest" stuff that a lot of people had, but the shadow man would always approach from outside my door. Slowly getting closer to my bed. Slowly. Surely. I'd internally scream, struggle, do my best to move, run, alert someone, anything.

Yet there I lay. Motionless. Frozen. Nothing but my eyes able to move as this dark creature encroached on me. It never reached me. I always managed to wake up before it did. But that terror stuck with me, often for days, before I was finally able to sleep again.

It was a vicious cycle. I'd forget about it for months at a time and then I would happen again. Once it happened, it would be constantly on my mind so it would keep happening, night after night, until it stopped again for no reason and then I'd forget about it. Wash, rinse, repeat.

Sleep paralysis sucks.

I moved into Higanbana Heights a few weeks back. A fresh start in the big city after my last job went topsy-turvy. I'd long wanted to move to Tokyo and had been saving for it for years. The bust up at work with the moron who couldn't keep his mouth shut and yet got *me* fired was the final push I needed. I packed my bags, found the cheapest apartment I could, and off I went.

But then it started again. I hadn't even been here three days when I woke up, unable to move. My eyes instinctively moved to the door, where my usual shadow man approached from. It took me a moment to realise where I was and what was going on. Here's the thing. Even when you realise it's sleep paralysis—and you don't always realise, even years later—that doesn't make it any less terrifying.

I lay in bed, staring at the door. Sweat poured down my brow. I could feel it. It's the strangest sensation when you can't move, and yet you can feel the actual beads of sweat running down your face. Another thing they didn't mention about Tokyo. It was so damn hot during summer.

Anyway, I lay there, looking at the door and the familiar ball of terror in my chest grew bigger and bigger. It's coming. It followed me all the way there. I didn't actually know whether the shadow man that haunted my paralysis was the same being created by my mind or there were a variety of them. Did it matter? I knew it was all in my head, the shadow man wasn't real, and yet I was terrified all the same.

I waited for the door to creak. I preemptively struggled, thinking maybe this time I could get the jump on him. He wouldn't get me this time. He? She? It? Whatever it was, I was a full-grown adult now. It couldn't keep scaring me like this.

Yet the door didn't creak, and it didn't slip past the end of my bed, sidling up beside me and looking down upon my terrified face as I was forced to also look upon it.

No. Because it was already in the room. My eyes flickered to the corner and I could have sworn my heart was going to burst in terror. He wasn't coming through the door because he was already here. In the corner. Standing there watching me. Didn't move, didn't approach me, didn't do anything. Just watched. At least, I assumed that was what it was doing. Kinda hard to tell when it had no facial features. Just a void in my already dark room, vaguely shaped like a human.

I tried to shut my eyes, but I couldn't. I stared at it as it stared at me. A face off I terribly wanted to break yet couldn't.

* * *

At some point morning had broken, and the thing was gone. Sunlight filtered in through the cheap curtains I'd taken from a tenant moving out and some birds chirped. Had I fallen asleep again? Or was I locked in such an intense battle with the thing that I entirely lost track of time?

Shortly after moving in, I started hearing rumours about Higanbana Heights. The building was haunted. People didn't tend to last long—for a variety of reasons. That was why the rent was so cheap. People avoided even passing it if they could, and many businesses had packed up shop and moved because they feared its influence.

Were the rumours true? Maybe. About a week back there was this horrible sound outside, I don't know how to describe it. Like smacking a nice big soft roast onto the counter. Splat. Thud. Hard but squishy, you know? It was quickly followed by another. I went over to the window to see what was going on and was just in time to catch a body flying over the edge.

Three of them, all dead in the parking lot after falling from the top floor. Or at least that was the story. I passed a couple whispering that they hadn't jumped, they'd been thrown. Their friend, the girl who lived here, seemed oddly unfazed by their deaths. Apparently they hung out here every weekend, to the extent that the other residents recognised them even though they didn't live here themselves.

Did she throw them over? Did they jump? Did it matter? They were dead and people claimed that the building had a hand in it. Stupid, right?

But as I lay in bed that very same night, staring at the shadow man in the corner, I wondered. My heart beat like a drum, throbbing in my ears, and I searched the room all over, wondering when he would make his move. But he didn't. He stood there. Watching me. As though he was waiting for something. I eventually fell asleep again, and when I woke up, he was gone.

Maybe it was a sign I was growing up. I recognised the demon and it no longer had any power over me. I'd done enough research that I knew it was just something my brain created. The shadow man wasn't real. It was, at best, an illusion. Not really a living dream, but that wouldn't be the worst way to explain it either. Dreaming while awake? Yeah, something like that.

As a kid, I had no idea. I just thought a demon or a ghost was tormenting me, trying to kill me, and it was succeeding. It spent many years destroying my life. It wasn't until later that I realised it was just a misfiring in the brain, but by that point, well, it was a little late to change the jumpy, angry person I'd become.

But now. See. It wasn't doing anything. I knew better. I was an adult. I understood the scientific reasons behind it. Now all it could do was watch me from the corner because, deep down, my brain understood. Who cared if the building was supposed to be haunted? Who cared if people avoided it? All the better for me! Cheap rent and no-one getting in my business!

At the end of the day, it was all in my head anyway.

* * *

Two nights ago, I woke up as usual and my eyes went straight to the corner. It wasn't there. I tried to smile, but of course I couldn't. Sleep paralysis. Yet I remained calm. Let logic guide me. My body just hadn't woken up yet, and my brain was a little confused. Just let it happen.

I soon realised the shadow man wasn't in the corner because he was beside my bed. I tried to scream, but nothing came out. It was a scream of surprise, and as much as I hated to admit it, a little terror.

I hadn't expected that. It had been so long since the shadowy figure had approached my bed, I'd almost forgotten that it even could. "What do you want?" I wanted to ask. "Leave me alone!" I wanted to scream. But that would be silly. For one, I couldn't talk, and two, it wasn't real. It felt real. Oh boy, did it feel real. But it wasn't. I knew that.

It stared at me with invisible eyes. I stared back at it. Usually at this point I would fully wake up and the shadow would disappear, but not this time. It stared at me, close enough that if I could reach out and touch it, I'd be able to brush my hand right through it. Was it solid? Would I hit it instead? I'd never had a good chance to look at it up close, and from this distance it looked kinda hazy. Not quite smoke, but not quite solid either.

A 3D shadow, lurking in the darkness.

I calmed my racing heart, closed my eyes, counted down from 10... and next thing I knew, it was morning. The shadow was gone.

Odd. That had never happened before. Maybe my own brain was upset that I was no longer scared by the creature it thought up and so was getting more creative. What an asshole. I refused to let it get to me. I was the one in control, not my stupid brain.

APARTMENT 308

* * *

Last night I stayed up late. I didn't want to admit it, but it had gotten to me. I just wanted a good night's sleep. Why couldn't I have that? It seemed like nearly every night I spent in this apartment, something happened. Maybe it was the stress of the move and the stress of trying to find a new job. Maybe my brain was just fucked in its wiring and would be like this always. Luck of the draw and I lucked out.

I drank the most bitter, foul tasting coffee I could afford and eventually passed out on the couch sometime before the sun rose. If there was a shadow man, I didn't see him. But I also woke up feeling like even worse shit than if I had.

So, that was that. Spend my life avoiding sleep again, or just ride this particular bout out. They never tended to last long, and once it stopped, I could expect to be paralysis-free for at least a few more months before it might happen again. Yeah. I could do that.

Couldn't I?

* * *

After yet another day of doing sweet fuck all, I climbed into bed. Part of me wanted to spend the night on the couch again, drinking swamp water and flicking through whatever shit was on TV, but another part of me hated my own brain and wanted to show it who was the boss. If stubborn had a picture in the dictionary, it was of me.

That stubborn part won, because at some point I woke up, unable to move. 'Ah, here we go again...' My eyes went straight to the corner of the room, and as I suspected, nothing there. They took a moment to adjust, and then I screamed when I saw it. Or at least, I tried to scream. Internally I did, but no voice came out. Not even a whimper.

The shadowy figure stood over me, right by my pillow, looking down at my face. I thrashed and struggled, at least in my head, but my body refused to obey my commands. The figure had never gotten this close before. If I could have moved, I could have bopped it with my nose.

'It's not real,' I reminded myself, yet my entire body screamed in fear. No, it's not real, but it looks and feels pretty fucking real. It had no face that I could discern, and yet I could feel it looking at me, blinking, breathing, taking me in. Thinking. Considering. Watching. Examining. Plotting.

'Leave me alone!' I wanted to scream. 'Why won't you just leave me the hell alone?'

Should have drank the sludge water. Should have watched TV. Should have done anything but fallen asleep in this shitty old bed where I knew I'd see this again.

Something cold gripped my ankle. My heart skipped a beat. The thing was right beside me, so it couldn't be that. I looked down, but I couldn't see a thing. Only my twisted blankets and leg sticking out.

The blankets by my legs depressed, as though something had jumped on the bed. I looked back and the figure was gone. It was... on top of me.

Climbing up the bed. Drawing closer to my hips, my chest, my face. How had it...? What?

It didn't make sense. Of course it didn't. I wasn't awake. Not fully. Breathe. How do you usually get out of this?

The figure had never made it this far before. It usually disappeared before ever reaching the bed. I'd gotten so used to it over the years that even in a panicked state I was able to wake myself up before that ever happened.

'Wake up!' I screamed inside. 'It's just a dream! Wake up!'

A terrifying chill settled over me. What if this wasn't a dream? What if this figure was actually real? I'd been ignoring it all this time, attributing it to my usual sleep paralysis, but what if... it wasn't?

A whole new fear washed over me. I renewed my attempts to struggle, yet nothing happened. The figure climbed higher and higher, finally resting above my face. I squeezed my eyes shut, unable to look at it any longer. Its hands pressed down beside my arms, its legs rested on either side of my hips. If it could breathe, I'd no doubt be feeling its breath on my face at that very moment.

I couldn't open my eyes. I refused to look at it. My heart pounded so fast I feared it was about to run out of steam and stop. Maybe that would be for the best. Then I wouldn't have to find out whatever that thing on top of me was. Whether this was really a waking dream or not.

Thoughts ran through my head too fast to keep up. It's just a dream. Just a hallucination. No, it's real. You can feel the pressure of it on top of you.

You felt the icy cold grip on your ankle. You felt it looking right at you. You've never had that before. This is different. This is new. No, it's just the usual dream developing, playing out further than you've ever let it before. It's nothing to be afraid of. Just open your eyes.

Open your eyes.

Open them!

I opened them and screamed. My entire body flailed, and I kicked the shadow off me. I fell out of bed, scrambling to the wall and hitting my head against it as I tumbled. The figure stood on the other side of the bed, staring at me. I looked down at my hands, as though seeing them for the first time.

I was awake. I could feel, I could move. My head pounded. I could feel pain. And yet…

It was still there. The shadow man looked at me from across the bed. My stomach sank.

It was real. It wasn't a dream. All this time I'd ignored it, let it get closer and closer, all because I thought it was just another sleep paralysis dream.

What a fool I'd been.

Now it had reached me. It had touched me. Its intentions were clear as day, and they weren't friendly. I felt it the first time I saw it. A simmering rage. A barely hidden malice. I felt it even stronger when it gripped my ankle with an icy hand.

It wanted me dead. It wanted me out of its space. This apartment belonged to it, and I wasn't welcome.

The shadow stood between me and the door. I'd never make it. The window above my head was ajar, but I didn't like my chances of surviving the drop, if I could even reach it in time.

So, this was how it ended. In a standoff with the shadow figure of my dreams. No, not my dreams. This was something else entirely. Anybody else would have noticed it right away and gotten the fuck outta here. Me? This wasn't my first rodeo. It would, however, be my last.

I had to run for the door. It was my only chance. I planted my hands on the wall behind me, slowly edging up until I stood. The shadow man matched me, rising to full height, the both of us standing on either side of the bed, looking at each other. He was closer to the door. He could cover that distance in an instant. But I had to try it. What other option was there?

I ran. No time to think. I moved, letting my body take over, seeing myself reaching for the door and sliding through it. Running down the hall towards the living room, flinging the door open, and escaping to freedom. It wouldn't follow me out there. Perhaps couldn't. Just get out. That was what it wanted all along. Get out. I'd been too dumb to hear it. Well, let me grant your wish.

Yet I didn't reach the door. My body stopped of its own accord, or at least it felt that way. I'd actually run into a wall of ice, an unnatural feeling in the sultry summer heat, and it gripped me tight. Icy cold fingers squeezed my arms as it held me, and I screamed. Not out of fear at seeing it up close, nor at disappointment in missing the door.

No. In terror at the sights it showed me. The walls turned red, streaking with blood. Screams not my own filled my ears, the screams of hundreds, perhaps thousands stuck in this one spot in pain, in agony, unable to break free of the walls trapping them. The building... the building was Hell itself. There was no escape, not now, not ever.

The anger, the hatred emanating off the shadow terrified me, but it wasn't for reasons I had suspected. I was *alive*. It hated me because I was alive. I was here, living and breathing, able to come and go as I pleased and I chose to stay. All it wanted was to be free. To move on to the other side.

Yet it couldn't. The building kept it here, along with all the others. They were trapped. Their spirits forever crying in agony, wanting to break free but tied here by some unknown power. No Shinto priest or Buddhist monk could free them. Many had tried. All had failed. Some had even joined them.

Warm liquid swelled over my feet. I knew what it was without seeing it. I could smell it. Blood. Blood like that staining the walls, the roof, the bed, the closet, the window. It stank in the putrid heat, and yet the icy cold grip on my arms held me tight.

'You understand now, don't you?' it seemed to say. It had no face. Perhaps it had been here so long that it didn't even remember what it looked like in life. Time had carved away at its face, its features, its uniqueness, until it no longer remembered what it once was. A man? A woman? A teacher? A mother? A scientist? A folklorist? A simple villager? A soldier? It no longer remembered. Too much time had passed, and unlike those it had once known, spirits of friends and loved ones that had moved on to the other side long ago, it remained trapped here, a rotting spirit turned black with decay.

And it couldn't stop itself. Didn't want to stop itself. It was in so much pain that this was the only way it could react.

The blood continued to rise. It covered the bed and drenched my thighs. Soon it would reach the open window. Would it start pouring out? Or was it all in my head? An illusion brought on by the hungry shadow in front of me.

Did it matter?

It warned me. Over and over. And I ignored it. I had my chance to leave, like any normal person would have done seeing a shadowy creature in the darkness of their bedroom. Yet I remained. I had no one to blame but myself.

I screamed. I screamed as loud as my lungs would allow as it dragged me down. Down into the blood.

Down into Hell.

APARTMENT 702

WHAT WAS HER NAME? WHERE did she come from? What did she do? Did she live alone? Did she have a pet? What type of movies did she like?

Questions swirled through my head as I looked up at her again. Work kept me late most nights, meaning the city was quieter than usual by the time I got home, and the apartment building even more so. It was quiet at the best of times, but once night fell, it was like a veil fell with it and it withdrew into its own world.

She first caught my eye several nights earlier. I parked my car and got out and saw her standing by her window, looking out at the stars. She lived on the seventh floor, while I lived on the second. Yet something about her drew me to her. The soft paleness of her skin. Her immaculately done hair. Her never-ending gaze into the stars, both whimsical and romantic at the same time.

She was beautiful. I wanted to get to know her,

to find out what she was looking at, to understand what drew her to stand by that window for what felt like hours on end just looking into the sky. What was she thinking? Was she thinking anything? Or was she just... letting go. Freeing herself of human thought and problems and letting the cosmos fill her with freedom. Freedom born of the knowledge that she was but one woman on an insignificant speck of dust in a universe far too large for the human mind to comprehend.

I saw her again the following night, and then the night after that as well. Standing by the same spot, staring into the sparkling sky. Her beauty entranced me, like the stars entranced her. I sat in my car, perhaps watching her for longer than was healthy, and then finally moved inside once the growling of my stomach got too much to bear.

I ate dinner alone, the clock ticking closer and closer to midnight. I'd never felt this way before. It was strange. Normally, work consumed my every living thought, and often my every waking minute. As an accountant for an upcoming firm in Tokyo, I wasn't exactly the highest paid businessman around, but I did okay. I'd saved and worked hard enough that, if I wanted, I could move out of this shitty old building and into a better apartment near work. Pamphlets on the table reminded me of several buildings I hadn't looked at yet.

And yet... here I sat. Thinking about a woman several floors above me that I didn't know and yet couldn't get out of my mind. The way she appeared so suddenly when I was thinking of moving seemed almost too much to be a coincidence. Like the building was trying to keep me here.

It sounded stupid even as I thought it, and certainly not something I would say out loud to anyone else, but deep in the back of my mind, the thought wouldn't go away. There was a reason I noticed her standing by her window. There was a reason that single act had forced me to question whether I wanted to move or not. Something wanted me to stay. To get to know that woman. To find out her story, to tell her my story, to live happily ever after in a city full of eternal strangers.

Ah. I let my thoughts get away from me again. But still. My brain scrolled through countless ways to try to introduce myself to the woman sometime. I had to meet her for real. I couldn't just keep staring at her from my car while she stood by her bedroom window looking outside. That was creepy. Even I recognised that.

But that still didn't answer the question of how. I couldn't just walk upstairs, knock on her door and be like, "Hey, so, I've seen you staring at the stars from your window. Wanna have dinner?" That was a quick visit to creepsville, and possibly the police station for being a stalker.

It had to be smooth, casual, and normal. Like bumping into her on the stairs one day as she was carrying her groceries up. No, that wouldn't work. She lived on the seventh floor. She'd use the elevator. Maybe running into her in the lobby downstairs when she was checking her mail. Or at the convenience store around the corner! I'd seen several other tenants there, especially late at night when other places weren't open.

A devious plan formed in my mind. The mail. Yes. I wouldn't have to wait around for her to pick it up. There was no telling when she might do that, and standing by the mailboxes was more than a little creepy. But if, somehow, something meant for her accidentally got delivered to me instead, well, then I could take it up to her directly. Our apartment numbers looked very similar, after all. Easy to mistake 702 for 202.

"Hi, are you from 702? Of course you are, it says that on the front door. Anyway, I believe this belongs to you. It was accidentally delivered to my mailbox instead. I live just a couple of floors down. Would I like to come in? Oh, well, I mean, if you insist, sure, I'd love to. What a lovely home you have here, by the way... And I didn't catch your name..."

Ah. Again my mind ran off of its own accord, yet I couldn't wipe the grin from my face at the thought of it. It was perfect. Foolproof. It gave me a reason to see her, it gave me a reason to introduce myself and let her know that I lived in the same building, and it opened the way for us to get to know each other better. Who didn't love a helpful neighbour?

It just left one question. How to get her mail? I couldn't wait around for the mailman to make a mistake. I had to be proactive. Get a letter myself. The mailman often shoved letters and leaflets into the mailbox together, meaning, they didn't always go all the way in. That was it. Just snatch one as it poked out. It didn't matter what it was, as long as it had her address on it. It wasn't like I was stealing it.

I was merely giving it to her in person. A little extra service.

'Thank god for the mailman's laziness.' It was too perfect. I gobbled down the rest of my cooling bento box from the convenience store and then hit the shower. Satisfied dreams would fill my sleep that night, no doubt about it.

* * *

I checked the mailbox on my way to work the next morning, but I couldn't see anything sticking out. The mailman didn't arrive till around lunchtime, so of course it was too early.

When I got home that night, however, it was another story. I watched her from my car again, memorising what I could of her face from a distance. Elegant cheekbones, big round eyes, dark red lips and pale skin. I'd never seen a more pure vision of beauty in my life. Yeah, sure, she was far away, she might look different up close, but something told me that wasn't the case. She was a true beauty, and not even seven floors could obscure that.

And as I entered the lobby, I saw it. A big fat wad of mail poking out of the box labelled 702. This was it. Like the world knew my intentions and was helping me out. I was supposed to do this. Fate was giving me a helping hand. It couldn't be any more obvious. Why, fate might have been the very thing to plant the idea in my head in the first place. The greatest love stories were always brought together by fate, were they not?

I smiled, pinching a letter and quickly shoving it into my jacket. I ran upstairs with glee and flung my door open.

"Alright. Calm down." I kicked the door closed behind me and dropped my suitcase off on the coffee table. I had it in my hands. Mail for 702. I took it out of my jacket with a trembling hand and, for the first time, laid eyes upon her name. Finally, a name to go with the face.

Hoshino Ami. Oh. It was too good. Too perfect. There were even stars in her name. What a beautiful name for a beautiful woman. Like her parents knew the day she was born that her beauty would rival that of the stars themselves. That people would look up at her, like she looked up at them, and marvel at her radiance.

I held the letter close to my chest and took a deep breath, letting it all fill me. Fate was a cruel master sometimes, but in that very moment, everything had fallen into place. It was meant to be. Now, I just had to go up there and grab it.

And so I did. I pressed the button for the elevator and waited an excruciatingly long time for it to come down. As I stepped inside, I realised I'd never even used the elevator before. It played boring, not even cheerful music as it rose to the designated seventh floor. I stepped out, and a cool breeze washed over my face. It felt nice in the summer heat. Another sign that this was meant to be.

My heart pounded as each step took me closer to my goal. Towards her. This was it. The big moment. Finally we would meet face to face and I would get to see her beauty up-close.

Hoshino Ami. Again the name sparked to life in my head. A perfect name for a perfect woman. Was she standing by her bedroom window at that very moment, still looking at the stars she got her name from? Was it that aspect alone that had given her an interest in them? There were so many things I wanted to know about her.

I stopped before her door. 702. It looked the same as every other apartment in the building. I held the letter in one trembling hand and raised the other to knock. Not the doorbell, that was too impersonal. A gentle but solid knock. Three times. Enough to let her know there was important business at the door, yet not too much to be annoying or set her on edge.

Alright. Time to take what fate had granted me.

One. Two. Three. Three solid knocks. I took a step back and held the letter with two nervous hands. I glanced at my watch. 10 p.m. Well, it was a little late for a door-to-door salesman, maybe, but not a neighbour.

A minute passed. Then another. No response. My heart pounded so hard it threatened to break free of my rib cage. No. It wasn't supposed to go like this. She was supposed to open the door, see me, and invite me in with open arms. I had her mail. Fate had conspired to make sure this happened.

Furrowing my brow, I knocked on the door again. Same as before. Three gentle but firm knocks. I took another step back, but this time the door to 701 opened.

"Hey, it's 10 p.m. What the hell are you doing?" It was a young man, shirtless and his hair ruffled.

"None of your business," I said, giving him a quick once over. A junkie, maybe. Probably some type of bum that didn't deserve to be living next to this gorgeous, perfect woman.

"Well it is my business when you're banging at all hours of the night. It's late. Fuck off and come back tomorrow. I haven't seen her for a while anyway, she probably fucked off like everyone else has been."

I raised an eyebrow. "You... haven't seen her?" But... I'd seen her just 10 minutes earlier. I'd watched her from my car. She was definitely there, standing by the window and looking out as usual.

"Nah man, it's been all quiet there for the last week or so. She was making an awful racket that night, I had to bang on the walls to shut her the fuck up. If you're after money or something, you're shit outta luck, mate."

"I'm not... after money..." I couldn't stop my voice from sounding indignant and childlike. Petulant. Ugh. Who on earth was this man and why was he so disrespectful of others?

"Sure, whatever, just shut the fuck up, I'm trying to sleep, okay?" He closed the door with a bang and I was left alone on the balcony once more.

Still. Odd. Very odd. I had seen her just a few minutes ago. Yet she wasn't answering the door, and according to her slovenly neighbour, he hadn't heard anything coming from the apartment for the last week.

I raised my hand to knock again, but then thought better of it. For whatever reason, tonight wasn't supposed to be the night. Maybe she was asleep. Yeah, that was it. She had earplugs or some noise cancelling headphones on or something and just couldn't hear the knocking at the door. Of course. It made perfect sense. I didn't know why I hadn't thought of it sooner. She was asleep. That was all.

I'd try again the following night. I'd just have to be a little earlier this time. As soon as I saw her in the window on my way back, I'd rush right upstairs. No hanging around watching her this time. Our shared time together as she looked at the stars and I looked at her would be sacrificed, but it would be worth it.

* * *

Work passed so slowly the following day that I feared fate was playing with me. The usual overtime request came in right as the clock was about to hit home time, and I agreed for only one reason: she wouldn't be standing by her window if the stars weren't out yet.

Why that mattered, I wasn't so sure. But she no doubt had work as well, and it would be creepy to hang around her front door for hours waiting for her to get back. I took on the work, pretended to do things while I shuffled papers around, and then as soon as I saw the sky darkening outside, I took off.

She was there. My heart pounded like a jackhammer. 8 p.m. The earliest I'd been home in weeks, and still she was standing at her window, looking outside. How long did she stare at the stars for each night? I couldn't remember a time seeing her go to bed before me. Maybe she was a scientist? Or maybe she had a lot on her mind.

Hoshino Ami. All of my questions would soon be answered. I almost skipped over to the elevator and pressed the button. Seventh floor, here I come.

The same tune as the night before played as the elevator rose all too slowly. I stepped out after an eternity, fixed my tie, adjusted my hair, and pulled the letter out of my bag. Alright. Here we go!

I walked over and knocked on the door. Three nice, strong knocks. At this very moment she should have been standing by her bedroom window, looking outside. I wanted to make sure she could hear it.

I waited. No response. Odd. I raised my hand and knocked again. One minute passed. Two minutes passed. A chilly breeze blew through my hair, as though running its cold tendrils through it. Why wasn't she answering?

Then it hit me. Ah, it all made sense now. She was deaf. She no doubt stared out her window day in, day out because it gave her a sense of peace. She couldn't hear my knocking because she couldn't hear anything. There was no other way to explain it.

Something nearby caught my attention. "...Oh?" The window was ajar. Not enough for outsiders to see, not unless they were right in front of it, but it wasn't closed all the way.

Desperate times called for desperate measures. I was sure she'd forgive a little intrusion if I explained it to her. Fate had conspired to bring us together, after all. I didn't speak sign language, but we'd find a way. Maybe she could read lips? Her own dark red lips came to mind, and I swallowed. She was just a few metres away, a few walls and windows keeping us apart.

Not any longer.

Checking to make sure no-one else was around, I slid the window open and jumped inside. There was a dull, dank odour that permeated the dark living room, almost too dark to see. A few flies buzzed around something in the kitchen, trash probably. Ah, that would explain it. There were still two more days till trash day, and the old lady downstairs got real upset if you took anything down beforehand. Still, she could have put it out on the balcony or something. Maybe the smell of it wafted towards her bedroom while looking outside?

I cleared my throat. "Ahem. Hello?" No need to frighten the poor woman any more than she was likely going to be. Maybe she wasn't really deaf but hard of hearing, or so lost in thoughts that she didn't hear my knocking. So many uncertainties.

The apartment seemed to beckon me in, pulling me closer to her room. The layout was the exact same as mine, so finding my way down was easy. No doubt all the apartments in the building had the same basic layout. Living room and kitchen at one end, a tiny hall leading to two rooms and a bathroom at the other. Only a door stood between me and her now. One single door keeping me from my fate.

I closed my eyes and took a deep breath. Savour the moment. Everything changes after this. Finally, the woman of my dreams was about to be mine. Or, at the very least, the first steps taken. I smiled.

Always getting ahead of myself. We still had to introduce ourselves to each other first.

A familiar smell pierced my nostrils, emanating from Ami's room. I took a deep breath and cringed. Was there trash in her room as well? That didn't seem very healthy. Nothing wrong with putting that on the balcony, despite what the neighbours may say. I raised my hand to knock and then thought better of it. I'd come this far. She hadn't heard my first knocks. No point drawing this out any longer than I had to.

I gripped the door handle, steeling myself, allowing the moment to wash over me and basking in the fact that everything was about to change. Here it was. The one single moment that would change my life forever. I twisted the handle and swung the door open.

I wasn't quite sure what I expected to see before me, but it wasn't this.

Nothing. There was... nothing. No bed. No clothes on the floor. No woman standing by the window.

Absolutely nothing.

No. I shook my head. This didn't make sense. I saw her. She was standing by that window when I parked downstairs only a few minutes earlier. There was no way she could have left the house in that time without me seeing her. And... and that didn't explain why the room was empty anyway!

I stepped inside and almost gagged. Ugh. The smell was so much stronger in here. I took a tentative step towards the window, and then another. It felt like stepping on sacred ground. I didn't deserve to be here, but I couldn't stop myself either. This was the very spot she should have been standing on. The same spot I saw her from, night after night, staring wistfully into the sky.

Yet I couldn't help myself. I wanted to see the same view she had. The stench made me want to lose my lunch, but it would only take a moment. A shared view that only the two of us understood. I stepped up to the window and placed my hands on it, sticking my head outside.

Stars… kind of. Countless shining balls of light in the sky, mostly obscured by buildings and the harsh lights of the city. It… wasn't a very nice view. In fact, you could barely see any stars at all. A few here and there, sure, but…

Odd.

The front door slammed and I jumped. Shit. Someone was here! Had she really left the house while I was on the elevator and was only now coming back? What would she think if she came in and found a strange man in her bedroom? No. It wasn't supposed to go down like this!

I looked around, looking for a place to hide. There was nothing. Literally nothing. No bed. No anything. How was this even a bedroom? How did she live here?

…What if it wasn't Ami whose footsteps I could hear coming down the hall? What if someone had kidnapped her! And taken all her stuff!

I had to hide. I couldn't let them see me. There was only one place: the closet.

I reached for it and stopped. There was a voice on the other side of the door. A female voice.

"Look, I told you, I took care of it! Yeah. Yeah. She's gone. I've been waiting for the heat to die down before I move her. This place fucking stinks. Glad I moved all my shit out first, or I'd have to replace it all. I didn't plan on being here for this long, but ah well, you gotta deal with the hand fate deals ya, huh? Uh huh. Uh huh. I'll be dumping the body tonight, I'm just grabbing her. Uh huh. Yeah, that swamp down by Inoto Park. Nobody goes there anymore, people say it's haunted or some shit. Once she's gone, I'm outta here for good. I hate this fucking place. Nah man, I don't believe in ghosts, but you try living here surrounded by freaks and cops and weird shit at all hours of the night. I need my beauty sleep. Uh huh. Uh huh. Alright. Look, I'll call you back once it's done. I just wanna get the fuck outta here. I'm never coming back to this shithole again."

Trying to process everything I'd just heard, I turned back to the closet and found myself face to face with someone all too familiar.

My heart stopped.

"Ami?"

"Help me."

Blood streaked her pale face, staining her tattered clothes. Her pale skin was white; not the type of white from someone who has spent their life indoors avoiding sunlight, but *white*. Like a blank canvas white. The whites of her eyes were stained red and as she opened her mouth again, a terrible gurgle erupted from it.

I screamed and fell backwards. The bedroom door flung open and a woman with short hair stood there, her phone in hand and a confused, angry expression on her face.

"Who the fuck are you?"

"Who the fuck are *you*?" I repeated the question.

"This is my fucking apartment, so I'm the one who should be asking that!"

Her... apartment? I turned back towards the closet and Ami... the woman... was gone.

"...Ami?"

She narrowed her eyes. "How the fuck do you know my name?"

She certainly had a potty mouth. With a trembling hand, I held a letter up. "I... uh... this was... delivered to me... by mistake..."

This wasn't my Ami. My beloved Hoshino Ami who stared at the stars with a whimsical look on her beautiful, delicate face. This woman was anything but delicate.

She snatched it out of my hand and then pulled a gun from the back of her jeans.

"Hey, whoa, calm down!" I scooted back to the wall and held my hands in the air.

"You snooping through my mail? You some kinda weird pervert, huh?"

Something creaked nearby, but the woman continued her rant.

"Fuckers like you are exactly why I wanted out of this place. Fuck. It's just weirdos banging on the walls all night, footsteps running up and down the balcony and roof at all hours. Freaks watching you a little too long when you get in the elevator or—" she held the letter up as though to prove her point "—when you're just trying to get your damn mail."

The creaking got louder. I was pretty sure I'd wet myself with the gun in my face and all, but the creaking wouldn't stop. I turned my head to see what it was, nausea rising in my stomach, and almost screamed again.

"Hey, are you listening to me, you dumb fuck?"

My mouth opened and closed. No sound came out. The closet door slid further and further across.

"The fuck are you looking at?" The woman... Ami... the real Ami... looked between me and the closet door, her brow furrowing.

"Y-You don't see that?"

"See what?" She grew even more confused. I tried to point at the door, but my hand was shaking too much to be of any use.

"T-The door... it's..." It opened. And inside it, a body lay slouched on the ground. Skin pale, dried blood stuck to its face. A single bullet wound in the head.

Ami. *My* Ami. The woman I'd seen by the window, staring at the stars night after night. Only... she wasn't Ami. She didn't live here. The woman with the gun at my face did. She had killed her and brought her body here. Probably around the first time I saw her.

My beautiful Ami. She... she was dead all along. I was never going to be in time for her. It was too late from the very beginning. Fate truly was a cruel mistress, laughing at me somewhere over how this series of events had played out.

"Help... me..." That gurgling sound again.

"Y-You're already dead!" I tried to shuffle back, but my body wouldn't obey my commands. The dead body shifted, turning with a slow, jerky motion to look right at me. She fell to all floors and started crawling towards me.

"Oh what the fuck?" Ami, the real Ami, jumped back. "How the fuck are you not dead yet?" She coughed, covering her mouth. "Oh god, that stench…"

She was dead. She was very dead. I screamed as her cold hand tightened around my ankle.

No. It wasn't supposed to end like this. The woman of my dreams. We were supposed to run off and live happily ever after!

"Help…" Her words were cut off by another gurgle and by the sound of my own screaming. She yanked and pulled me towards the closet, moving so fast that I had no chance to grab anything… not that there was anything to grab in the empty room. The closet door slammed behind me and darkness filled my vision.

Well, almost.

The woman's corpse stared at me in the darkness, her eyes red and wide open. I fumbled for the door, my own screams filling my ears, but something was keeping it shut. I had a fair idea of what.

She was lonely. She wanted someone to find her. Whether she died in this very room or not, I couldn't tell. That would make the most sense, though. Left here, abandoned by her murderer, her friend, perhaps, a colleague, an enemy, whatever relationship they had, Ami, the real Ami, killed her and abandoned her body in her own closet. She'd already begun moving out, so it was the perfect place to leave her while she worked on plans for dumping the body.

But she hadn't counted on me seeing her. On this woman, I didn't even know her name, standing by the window, her silent call for help.

A call I had answered.

A call I now deeply regretted.

She couldn't be helped. She was already dead. No. Now she wanted company.

And I was to be that company. I'd fallen for it, hook, line, and sinker.

Everything fell silent. I realised I wasn't screaming anymore. I couldn't scream anymore.

Darkness flooded my vision. The world grew hazy. My consciousness faded in and out.

The last thing I saw was her chilling grin smiling down at me as the void swallowed me whole.

Her company had arrived. We would be together.

Forever.

APARTMENT 206

4:09 A.M. THAT WAS THE time the phone rang every morning.

"They're coming." That was all the voice on the other end would say.

They're coming. Who was coming? Who was calling me? Why was it at the exact same time every day?

Three weeks earlier, I moved into Higanbana Heights. Like most people living in the building, I didn't want to, but the rent was cheap and empty apartments abundant. You could have your pick of any floor. There were always a few empty apartments available on each. Tenants came and went faster than some people changed their underwear. Neither was healthy.

I, like many others, planned to stay only a short time. The apartments worked well as temporary housing, you had to give them at least that. Most apartments in and around Tokyo demanded a large deposit before moving in and also tied you to a two-year contract at the same time. If you wanted out before then, as most people did, then you had to pay a hefty fee to break contract and often lost your deposit at the same time.

Higanbana Heights? None of that nonsense. They were happy to get people in in the first place. You wanted to leave after a few weeks? Sure, at least you'd paid a month's worth of rent. It was more than they would have had otherwise. It baffled me how the building stayed in business, but considering how rundown it was and the constant stream of people in and out, well I suppose they made money somehow.

But this... This was not in the contract. I, like everyone else, had heard the rumours of the place. A gathering spot for ghosts, demons, murderers, addicts, the scum of both this world and the next. That was the *real* reason nobody lasted long.

Looking at the place, I could believe the murderers and addicts. I was fairly certain I'd passed a few on my way in and out of the building each day, but ghosts? Demons? The place was a shithole, not haunted. Who on earth believed in ghosts these days?

And yet... 4:09 a.m. On the dot. Every morning. The same voice, almost like a recording. "They're coming." The first time it happened, I mumbled and hung up. By the time I later woke up, I wasn't sure that it had even happened and suspected that I had dreamt it.

The second time it woke me up again, but this time I was more lucid. "Who is this?" I asked, but the phone hung up. The third night, same deal. "What do you want?" I screamed, but the other end hung up.

They never stuck around to chat. I never got anything out of them. I couldn't even be sure there was a person on the other end. It could have been a robo-call, set up to dial my number automatically and play back a tape.

"They're coming."

The biggest question was: why? Who would go to all of that trouble to bother me, a part-time supermarket worker studying to become a nurse? I didn't have any debt. I didn't have any enemies that I was aware of. I wasn't even from Tokyo. Like most other people, I'd ended up here because I was a countryside kid with big dreams but little money.

And, supposing that I even did have any enemies or people who wanted to scare me... why? That question wouldn't go away. Why go to all that trouble? What was the goal? The purpose? What were they hoping to achieve? Get me out of the apartment? Annoy me to death? What?

The calls especially annoyed me because the combination of work and study often left me hitting the sack late into the night. I was only hitting my first or second sleep cycle by the time it rang, disrupting me and then keeping me from getting back to sleep again because it was always on my mind. That and the summer heat. The building was so humid, even with the window open it just let more hot air in, and living on the second floor in Tokyo, well, it still wasn't very safe to leave the window open at night anyway.

I climbed into bed and looked at the clock. 3 a.m. I threw my head down on the pillow and let the soft mattress suck me in, a sigh of exhaustion escaping my lips. Assuming I could fall asleep right away, that meant barely an hour of sleep before the call would come.

A light bulb went off over my head and my eyes shot back open. Of course. Why hadn't I thought of it sooner? I grabbed the phone cord and yanked it from the wall. Done. No connection, no way to get through. My parents had my mobile number if there was ever an emergency taking place during the night that absolutely needed my assistance, but why did I even have a home phone in the first place? Not like I needed it for anything. It came with the internet so I accepted it, but I didn't actually use it.

Exhaustion had really done a number on me. How had I not thought of that? I smiled as I lay my head back down on the pillow and let blissful, uninterrupted sleep claim me.

It wasn't to be. Of course it wasn't. The clock flashed 4:09 a.m. as the phone rang, ripping me from a dream about a supermarket full of cheese. "Hello?" I answered automatically.

"They're coming."

I sat up in the bed. Before I had the chance to say something back, the phone hung up. I grabbed the phone line and yanked it. It wasn't plugged in. Memories of unplugging it before I fell asleep flooded back, and a chill ran down my sweaty spine.

It was unplugged. Yet it rang. I got the call. Same as always.

What on earth was going on?

* * *

I moved the phone to the spare room the next night. I covered it with a towel, closed the door, returned to my bedroom and closed that door too. Dreams of old teachers and unfinished tests haunted my mind until I was, once again, ripped forcefully from them.

The phone was ringing. The unconnected phone in another room hidden under a towel was ringing loud enough to wake me in my bedroom.

"No!" I buried my face under my pillow. No way was I going to answer it. Let it ring out. Let me sleep.

Yet it rang. It rang and it rang and it rang. After what felt like an eternity, I finally got out of bed. "Fine! You want me to answer? I'll answer!" I flung my door open and stormed into the spare room, picking up the receiver.

"What?" I screamed.

"They're coming."

I threw the phone back down, not worrying to put the receiver back in its place, and stormed back to bed. A shadow out the corner of my eye stopped me for a moment, but when I turned to look, there was nothing there.

"I hate this place," I muttered and waited for sleep to claim me again. Whoever was coming was only going to find a grumpy, sleep-deprived husk of a person at this rate.

Later that morning I found a note slipped under

the front door. *"Can you keep it down in the mornings, please? You're disturbing our sleep."* All I could do was laugh. I was disturbing *their* sleep? I knew it was that old bag, Ito. She was the only person in the entire building nosy enough to bother writing a letter to someone and then anonymously slipping it under their door. Maybe I should leave the phone by her front door before I went to bed.

I straightened up. Hey. That actually wasn't a bad idea. I let the thought linger as I got ready for work. She wanted noise, I'd give her some noise.

* * *

As the clock struck 2 a.m., I snuck into the spare room. I didn't know why I was sneaking in my own house, but that was the mood, I supposed. The phone hadn't been plugged in for days, and yet every night it still rang. At some point I stopped caring about the strangeness of it all and just grew more and more annoyed with it.

Sending me an anonymous letter because *she* was hearing noise? She wasn't the one having her sleep interrupted without fail every single morning! Well, she would be now. I stuck my head out the front door. All clear. You might expect that to be a normal thing at 2 a.m., but not at Higanbana Heights. The building seemed to come even more alive at night.

I ran past the stairs and gently placed the phone before her door. Making sure nobody was looking, I ran back to my own apartment and closed the door behind me with a soft *click*. Ah, the perfect crime.

Let her deal with the ringing and "they're coming" for once. Stupid cursed phone.

I collapsed into bed, a smile on my lips. Finally, time to get some real rest, and time for that nosy old bag to get some of what was coming to her.

* * *

A noise woke me up. I knew immediately what it was. It wasn't hard to guess. Again, the more important question was: why?

The phone. Ringing in the living room, by the sounds of it. I sat up and rubbed my eyes. Something in the corner of the room caught my attention, yet when I looked, it was gone. Poor sleep was messing with me again.

I stumbled down the hall and groped around in the dark. Finally my hands found it.

"Yes, I know…" I said, putting the receiver to my ear.

"They're coming."

I dropped the phone and fought the urge to cry. Why? Why was the phone back? Why wouldn't it leave me alone? I had put it outside, for the love of god, and yet here it was, back in my house again. The lock on the door was still locked, and the windows all shut tight. Old bag Ito couldn't have returned it; as much as she liked to masquerade that she had any authority here, she didn't, and she most certainly didn't have a key to get into other people's apartments.

I stumbled into the kitchen, opened the second drawer, and found what I was looking for. The hammer. Returning to the living room, I smashed the phone and the receiver, dropping the hammer and leaving the little bits of plastic and wire as I returned to bed. The room seemed darker than normal for this time of morning, but I didn't care. There. Call me now, I thought, as I waiting for another fitful sleep to claim me.

There was yet another note when I finally woke up a few hours later. *"If this noise keeps up, I'll be forced to lodge a complaint."* Lodge a complaint. Right up my ass. See if I cared. Pieces of the phone lay around the living room. I stepped around them as I got ready for work and rubbed my bleary eyes. Was it me or did the apartment still seem darker than usual? I looked outside; sunny. Hmm. Maybe I'd stressed my eyes too much with study and lack of sleep.

Leaving the phone where I'd destroyed it, I set out for yet another day of customers asking me questions they could answer themselves with half a second of thinking, and more medical terms than my mind knew what to do with. Only a few more months of this. It would all be over soon, one way or the other…

* * *

"What the…?" As I stumbled through the door past 9 p.m., I was not ready for the sight that greeted me in the living room. Nothing. Absolutely nothing. My shabby, dirty couch, a coffee table that was more of a crate with some textbooks on it, and… no phone.

I tilted my head. I distinctly remembered smashing it to pieces and leaving them where they fell when I left the house. Now... it was gone. I dropped my bag and headed straight for the bedroom, my heart rate spiking. It couldn't... No...

It had. There it sat. Atop the tiny bedside table. The phone, brand new, looking like it had just come off the assembly line, other than a slight yellowing of its white finish. A plug ran from it into the wall again.

"Oh hell no!" I tore it from the wall and tossed it into the spare bedroom again. "What the actual fuck?" Who was doing this? Why? Shadows seem to flee into the darkness as I searched the house. I knew full well I wouldn't find any people; the door was locked, the windows were shut, and nothing had been touched... nothing other than the phone.

The cursed phone! Why?

I collapsed onto the couch and held my head in my hands. Nothing worked. I destroyed the phone, and it just came back. My only way of escaping this would be to move out, and I didn't have the money for that yet.

Something moved out the corner of my eye. I turned towards the kitchen, but there was nothing but darkness. This lack of sleep was driving me nutty. Something else slipped by the door. I turned, but I was too late to catch it.

"What do you want?" I screamed, on the verge of tears. "What do you want..." I repeated, my voice dropping to a whisper. I had to study for my upcoming test, but I couldn't bring myself to do it. I was actually losing my mind.

They're coming. Let them come. I just wanted sleep. Blissful, quiet sleep...

I dragged myself to the bedroom, slammed the door behind me, and fell into bed.

*　*　*

A noise woke me up, but it wasn't the phone. Not this time. I clutched my blanket closer in the heat, hoping it might drown me, hide me, smother me, anything...

Voices. Voices woke me up, and as my eyes adjusted to the darkness, I realised I was no longer alone. Dark shadows surrounded the bed, peering down at me. They appeared to be talking to each other, and by the way they were gesturing and murmuring, it was about me.

I snatched a glance at the clock. 4 a.m. on the dot. Nine minutes until the phone rang. A chill washed over me. Had... had they always been there? Standing over me every night, watching me as I slept? They didn't seem to realise I was awake yet.

Clenching my eyes shut, I tried to listen to their voices over the sound of my own beating heart. I couldn't make anything out. It was gibberish, or not meant for human ears or something.

Who were they? What did they want? A cool touch brushed over my forehead and it took all I had not to whimper. Me. They wanted me. But why? What did they plan to do with me?

Another touch brushed my arm, and another my ankle. I couldn't move. Fear pinned me to the bed, and even if I wanted to scream—which I did—I couldn't.

I never believed the stories about Higanbana Heights. Not the supernatural ones, anyway. Regret fought with fear for dominance. All I wanted was to get my nursing degree and help people. The only way I could afford that was with cheap housing near my school. This place was perfect. I had ignored the rumours on purpose, even thanked them for making the rent so cheap.

What a fool I was.

Could I reach the door in time? What would they do if they realised I was awake? It hit me that all the strange shadows I'd seen around the house, the movement out the corner of my eye... it hadn't been my imagination. It wasn't my brain tricking me because I was tired.

It was them. They had been here the whole time. Watching. Waiting for something.

Something clicked in my brain.

Oh my god.

How had I missed it? The clock ticked closer towards 4:09 a.m. The same time I rang every morning, and for good reason. It was so simple. Not obvious, but so simple. So childishly simple.

The date.

We had just entered September. Today was September 4th.

They're coming. Today. On September 4th. 409. Whatever their plan was, they were carrying it out today. The phone hadn't been messing with me. It had been *warning* me.

I opened my eyes slightly, just enough to get the

gist of what was going on. Their conversation had picked up the pace, and several of the dark figures gestured towards the phone. They knew the time was coming. It would ring. It would wake me. They only had a few minutes at best to carry out their plan.

They didn't know I was awake yet. I wracked my brain for answers. Thinking with a cool, calm, rational mind was a challenge when all I wanted to do was scream and run.

September 4th. The date meant nothing to me, but it no doubt meant something to them. Assuming they were spirits, maybe it was the day they died? An anniversary of some kind?

Whatever. That didn't matter right now. The clock ticked. 4:08 a.m. One more minute. I had to make my move. They had to make their move.

Alright. This was it. I was going to make a run for it. Straight for the door. Move quickly and without warning. They'd be too confused to understand what was happening and I could use that to my advantage to escape.

I could do this. Psyching myself up, I clenched the blanket harder, my entire body tensing. Use this moment. Spring forth like a tiger. Spring forth to freedom.

The call was fast approaching. Now or never. Now or...

I couldn't move. I opened my eyes wide, and the dark creatures looked down on me. They seemed to smile in the darkness. I was frozen. Paralysed. A whimper escaped my lips, and they seemed to smile even harder.

My body jerked. The phone rang. It sent a jolt of fear through me, and the shadows turned to talk to each other, their voices rising in fear. Yes. Aha! You were too late as well! You had your chance, and you were too busy debating to take it! I tried to laugh, but I couldn't. I struggled to reach for the phone, but I still couldn't move.

Their feverish murmuring continued and a sickening realisation washed over me. It wasn't fear. They weren't afraid. They were excited. *This* was what that'd been waiting for. Dark tendrils extended around the phone and picked it up, placing it by my ear.

A familiar voice spoke.

"Welcome," it said, shifting into a horrendous laugh that filled the room. The dark creatures had joined it. It was a sound unlike any other I'd heard before, and filled me with a dread I'd never known.

"You've chosen to stay," it continued. "A brave choice. Soon our might will be strong enough to break free. To leave this cage. To roam free once more, like we used to, before…"

For a brief moment the shadows hovering above me seemed to take solid shape. Individual shape. A samurai. A thief. A ninja. A prince. A beggar. A professor. A doctor. People of varying ages, professions, and even eras. And as quickly as it came, it disappeared again. They were nothing but faceless, nameless shadows. A mass of energy, of rage, of malice, of hatred, vibrating with power. Joined together in a single goal.

To break free.

"We only needed one more. One strong enough

to help us push through. The bonds of this cage are far too strong for one alone to break free. Even together we have struggled, often limited to our own cages, unable to communicate. Unable to unite. Until tonight."

Their cages. The apartments? Something was keeping them here? What did that have to do with me?

"You might be wondering, 'why me?'" the voice continued, as though reading my mind. It was followed by a short, unpleasant laugh. "Nothing personal, but it has nothing to do with you. Not really. We simply needed one more soul strong enough to help us break free. Strong. Stubborn. Resilient. A soul with enough power to help push us over the edge. Years we have waited. Decades. For some, centuries."

The shadows watched over me in silence.

"The calls were a test, and congratulations, you passed! Most fled after a few nights, the strongest lasting perhaps a few weeks. We only get this one chance every year, and congratulations... you are the first in a decade to pass."

Why was it telling me this? What did they want from me? Why would I help them leave? That made no sense. And why was it on the phone?

Realisation washed over me again. The voices. The mumbling. They made no sense to me. Were they, the shadows standing above me, using the phone to communicate? Had they found a way through modern technology to reach me?

I wanted to laugh. The entire situation was so stupid, so ridiculous... Yet I was frozen to the bed, and I couldn't even scream, let alone laugh.

"Tonight, we break free, on this single day where the boundaries are thinnest. This cage will hold us no longer. We will be free to roam where we wish, do as we please, and it's all thanks to you..." The voice lowered and trailed off into a laugh. Adrenaline coursed through my veins, pumped harder and faster by the fear overwhelming me.

The dark figures closed in. The phone by my ear was gone. Maybe it hadn't even existed in the first place, a simple tool they had whipped up to reach me. It didn't matter.

I was frozen, prone on the bed, hot and sticky beneath the blanket while the blood in my veins chilled.

I tried to scream. No sound came out.

The shadows washed over me, dragging me down and down and down into the pits of despair. Of darkness. Of hatred. Of malice.

They brought me into them and images flashed through my mind too fast to keep up. Their memories. Their lives. The atrocities they committed. The hatred they felt. The wrongs done to them. Their grudges, bubbling beneath the surface for years, decades, centuries.

They didn't all die here. Some did, but others were called to the building, like many other monsters had been over the years. Wandering spirits without desire, summoned to this cage that bound and warped them, twisting them into the faceless, nameless creatures they now were.

Long ago, people had referred to the spot Higanbana Heights now stood on as the Gate to

Hell. They feared it. They stayed away from it. Yet as time passed, people forgot about it, and newer generations claimed that land to build their fancy new buildings on. Prime real estate in the big city couldn't be ignored, not even if that meant a few deaths every now and then.

But they hadn't foreseen what the building would become. Not only a death trap for the living, but a cage for the dead. Summoning evil of all sorts towards it. Murderers. Thieves. Spirits. Monsters. Some worked with it, able to come and go as they pleased, bringing more souls back to the building in exchange, but most... most were consumed by it. Trapped within its walls, forced to bide their time until they could break free. Their building rage and hatred warping them over the years, over the centuries, into something unrecognisable.

Something that wanted free. That wanted revenge.

Their joy rushed through me as they tore me apart, taking what they needed. My energy. My spirit. My goals. My desires. Everything. In an instant they took everything, leaving me as a shell of my former self. As one of them. Nameless. Formless. Filled with rage, hatred, and malice.

But that wasn't all. There was also... excitement. For the first time since being trapped in the building, they... no, we... were about to break free, and there was a big city out there just waiting for the taking.

The feeling as we broke free of Higanbana Heights for the first time, released into the cool air of the city and not the stifling heat that had consumed us for generations, was beyond liberating.

A giant city awaited us.
We were free.
We were hungry.
And we were coming.

WANT EVEN MORE?

Other series and books available from Tara A. Devlin:

Toshiden: Exploring Japanese Urban Legends

Reikan: The most haunted locations in Japan

Kaihan: Bizarre Crimes That Shook Japan

Kowabana: 'True' Japanese scary stories from around the internet

Aokigahara: The Truth Behind Japan's Suicide Forest

The Torihada Files

Read new stories each week at Kowabana.net, or get them delivered straight to your ear-buds with the *Kowabana* podcast!

ABOUT THE AUTHOR

Tara A. Devlin studied Japanese at the University of Queensland before moving to Japan in 2005. She lived in Matsue, the birthplace of Japanese ghost stories, for 10 years, where her love for Japanese horror really grew. And with Izumo, the birthplace of Japanese mythology, just a stone's throw away, she was never too far from the mysterious. You can find her collection of horror and fantasy writings at taraadevlin.com and translations of Japanese horror at kowabana.net.